LOST KITES
and
OTHER
TREASURES

ALSO BY CATHY CARR

365 DAYS TO ALASKA

AMULET BOOKS • NEW YORK

CATHY CARR

Cataloging-in-Publication Data has been applied for and may be obtained from the Library of Congress.

ISBN 978-1-4197-6799-9

Text © 2024 Cathy Carr
Book design by Deena Micah Fleming and Becky James

Scrapbook paper image by rawpixel.com on Freepik

Printed and bound in U.S.A.

10 9 8 7 6 5 4 3 2 1

Amulet Books are available at special discounts when purchased in quantity for premiums and promotions as well as fundraising or educational use. Special editions can also be created to specification. For details, contact specialsales@abramsbooks.com or the address below.

Amulet Books® is a registered trademark of Harry N. Abrams, Inc.

ABRAMS The Art of Books
195 Broadway, New York, NY 10007
abramsbooks.com

FOR BILL
FOR BILL KNOWS WHAT
AND BILL KNOWS WHY

and when we speak we are afraid
our words will not be heard
nor welcomed
but when we are silent
we are still afraid

So it is better to speak

AUDRE LORDE

"What makes the desert beautiful,"
said the little prince, "is that somewhere
it hides a well . . . "

ANTOINE DE SAINT-EXUPÉRY

They always say time changes things,
but you actually have to change them yourself.

ANDY WARHOL

CHAPTER 1

'M PUTTING AWAY MY lunch tray when I look outside and see something black and shiny jammed in the bushes.

Huh.

I walk over to the big sliding door that leads to our cafeteria patio and cup my hands around my eyes so I can get a better look through the glass.

Ruben Yao puts his lunch tray on top of mine and comes over to find out what I'm looking at.

"It's a garbage bag," he says.

Only it's not *just* a garbage bag. A bag would have more of a jellyfish shape. This mystery thing has sharp angles.

I open the door and head outside.

Ruben sighs and comes along. Ruben might not understand everything I do, but he always tries to be there for me anyway. That's one of the reasons he's my oldest best friend.

No one else is out here, because it's January. Freezing rain is spattering the benches and tables where everyone likes to hang in nicer weather.

Ruben rubs his hands together and folds his arms across

his chest. "Franny, couldn't we do this *after* school? When we have coats on?"

"Just give me a minute," I mutter, yanking on whatever it is.

I don't know if it'll still be here after school. It might blow away. Or one of the custodians might spot it. They don't always share my interest in found materials. A lot of people don't.

The mystery thing is made out of black trash bag plastic, like Ruben said, and it's really hard to pull out of the bush. That's because it's attached to a long piece of sewing thread, for some reason. That thread's gotten tangled up in leaves and branches. Once we break it off, we can finally tug the black plastic thing free and see that it's a kite.

It's not the kind you'd buy at a toy store—it's a homemade kite that someone made out of a heavy-duty garbage bag and some scrap wood. Its tail is more dusty plastic, torn into strips and knotted together. And the sewing thread? That's the kite string.

"What a piece of junk," Ruben says. "Do we toss it?"

From the way he says it, I can tell that's what he would do.

I hold up the kite and look at it again.

Sometimes when I find something, I have an idea about what to do with it right away. Like this big piece of bark I found last spring on my way home from school. I painted it on the smooth side with sunflowers, which are my nana's favorite flowers, and gave it to her for Mother's Day. She liked it. Nana doesn't like everything I make, but she liked that. She still has it propped up in her bedroom with the sunflower side facing out.

The bark was easy. I knew right away what I could do with it.

But other times it takes longer to figure out why some strange thing is tickling my brain. Maybe I should shove this bunch of plastic and splintery wood into the garbage can—but my art brain is telling me to hang on to it for a while. And Miss Midori, our art teacher and the Studio Club adviser, tells me to listen to that part of my brain. She says, "Franny, you can trust it."

"I don't know," I tell Ruben. "I think it's kind of cool."

"We could make something like that ourselves in about ten minutes."

"But we didn't," I say.

Ruben pulls the cafeteria door open just as the bell rings. He frowns. Ruben hates being late for class.

"You've got plenty of time!" I yell after him as he rushes off. "I'll see you later!"

"*You* better hurry," Ruben says before he disappears through the double doors.

He's not wrong. I rush down the hall to the art room and shove the kite into my cubby. I'm lucky it fits. Cubbies are designed for flat things, and a lot of the things I find aren't flat.

I give Miss Midori a quick wave, then speed-walk down the hall toward my math class. We get in a lot of trouble if the teachers catch us running.

I throw myself into my seat just as the bell rings.

Math is not my favorite class, and I'm not Mr. Winkler's favorite student, either. Today he's already scowling at me, which seems a little rude. I haven't even had the chance to say something dumb yet. Then he heaves one of the heavy sighs he saves up for when one of us disappoints him and says, "Frances Petroski."

I freeze.

I get called "Frances" when I've done something wrong. But what could that be? I'm not eating, talking, or using a phone. (I don't have a phone, so that one's easy.) I don't have my shoes up on the furniture, the way Aiden Houston does every class, but does Mr. Winkler ever even look in his direction? No, because Aiden is one of the kids at our school who's mastered the fine art of Getting Away With It.

"Could you come up here, please?"

When I'm at his desk, Mr. Winkler points at the clock over his head. All that tells me is that it's 12:05.

Finally he says, "Your appointment today. With Mr. Burns?"

"But that's Thursday, and this is . . . " I let my voice trail off while I think. "Wednesday?"

But no.

No, no, no!

I just had a tofu dog, chopped salad, and mandarin orange slices in the cafeteria, and that means *today* is Thursday.

"Sorry, Mr. Winkler."

Mr. Winkler sighs. "I'm sure he's waiting for you in his office. Franny, you *really* need to work on those executive skills. I'm going to drop your grandmother another note."

Oh great.

If there's one thing Nana doesn't like, it's emails from school.

I remind myself to add that to the list of Things Currently Worrying Franny Petroski.

I CAME HERE TO live with Nana the summer before kindergarten started. Back in those days, I had a lot of problems.

I lost my temper all the time and I couldn't stop crying once I started and I made things up. I also peed my pants a lot for a while. When I got stressed or nervous, that would happen.

When I started kindergarten, they pulled me out after a few months and sent me over to the pre-K instead. I had to do kindergarten the next year. Yeah, I flunked kindergarten.

I almost flunked second grade, too, when my teacher Mrs. Dixon didn't like me. She didn't like any of us, but she liked me the least. She always called me "Frances," like I was in trouble, and she picked at every little thing I did all day long. Mrs. Dixon made me so nervous, I could barely remember to raise my hand and ask to go to the bathroom, and I bet you can guess how that turned out.

Finally they took me out of Mrs. Dixon's class and put me

into Mrs. Shah's. Mrs. Shah smiled a lot and never raised her voice. She said I could go to the bathroom anytime I needed to—without asking first if it was an emergency. I liked her way more than Mrs. Dixon, and Mrs. Shah liked me, too. Kids can always tell when adults like them, and I think, if adults understood this, things might go along a lot more smoothly in the world.

Anyway, back in those days I had to see the school counselor all the time. But now I only check in once in a while. Like today, which is my beginning-of-term appointment. And they're saying next year maybe I won't have to do check-ins at all. I can just let Mr. Burns know if I need to talk about something.

Mr. Burns is our school counselor.

Mr. Burns is so skinny his clothes always look like they're about to fall off, and they're such weird clothes that some kids can't even look at him without laughing. He wears old slacks that are always covered with cat hair, wrinkled turtlenecks, and the same blue sports jacket every day. His beaky nose, the way he peers over his glasses, and the turtlenecks, they all come together to make him look like a turtle. Which is what a lot of the kids call him. But there's something about the slow way he blinks that makes me trust him. I also like the pictures of his cats, Toast and Bacon, that he keeps on his desk. I really want a cat, but our landlord doesn't allow animals.

I give a quick knock at his open door and he looks up. "Mr. Burns, I'm sorry! I thought it was Wednesday."

"Yesterday was Wednesday," Mr. Burns remarks. "Chicken tenders."

A Beyond Burger for me, because I'm a vegetarian. Still, I get the point. "I know, I remember now."

"Well, it's all right. You just keep working on that calendar awareness of yours. Come in and have a seat." Mr. Burns flips open a folder. He's old-fashioned like Nana. He fights with computers and he'd rather deal with paper. He leafs through my folder. "How was winter break? Did you do anything special?"

"Just the usual," I say. Nana and I, we do a lot of the usual. We have a routine. My grandmother likes routines.

"Okay. Well, we're almost halfway through the year. How are you feeling about sixth grade so far?"

Even someone like Mr. Burns asks a dumb adult question every once in a while.

How am I *feeling* about it?

It is what it is. That's what Nana says.

I go to class, I do my homework, I go to French language lab every week, and I'm working on multiplying fractions. I've learned where Madagascar is on a globe and that lemurs live there.

After school is pretty much the same every day too. I have Studio Club on Wednesdays, which is for art, and most other days I go to Homework Club, which is basically just a bunch of

9

us sitting in the cafeteria doing our homework, where there's good Wi-Fi and snacks and we can get help if we need it.

Then I walk home to my apartment. Nana and I eat dinner and after dinner I do more homework, or I draw or play around with art stuff. Lately I've been messing with this stuff called salt dough that you can mix up yourself at home, making little pinch pots and plaques. You might think it sounds like kindergarten, but if you've ever heard of Ruth Asawa, a famous sculptor, you may know she did a lot of cool things with salt dough. Sometimes Nana and I watch TV. Sometimes Nana goes to bed early, especially toward the end of the week when she's getting tired from work, and I just hang around by myself until it's late enough to go to bed.

On weekends I hang out with Lucy Bernal (my other best friend) or Ruben if they're not too busy with their families. If Ruben is free on Sunday afternoon, there are always board games at his house. The rest of the time I'm usually hanging around at home. I read or watch movies or do more art projects.

This is how Nana likes things. Nana calls this "comfortable." Or "relaxing."

And until sometime recently this was how I liked things too. I liked comfortable and safe. I liked predictable best of all. Nana said that made sense after the choppy-changey life I had with my mom, even though I was so little that I can hardly remember it. But lately sometimes I feel different about the way things always are with me and Nana.

Lately sometimes I feel flat. Or bored.

Or maybe, stuck.

Ruben and his family have this huge aquarium in their living room. I've always liked to watch all the action going on in there, but sometimes now I wonder how happy the fish are. I mean, they get food every day, and they're safe, but nothing ever changes, unless someone moves around the plastic plants. Ruben's mom, Dr. Yao, does that sometimes. She says it makes the fish think they're in a brand-new place. But sometimes it causes too much excitement, and then she has to change the plants back to where they were. Seriously, that's what she said.

Lately I feel like one of Ruben's fish.

Only, in my case, even the plastic plants don't get moved, because Nana likes them better where they are.

And she doesn't understand why I don't feel that way so much anymore.

Mr. Burns taps a pencil on his desk. "You looked deep in thought there, Franny. Do you want to share what you were thinking about?"

"Well . . . I guess sometimes I do get a little bored."

The moment the words are out, I wish I could call them back. I know I'm lucky to be where I am, with Nana.

11

"Maybe a few more activities would help with that. Did you ever talk to your nana about the French Club trip?"

Oh man! I wish I had never mentioned French Club to Mr. Burns. He's been making a big deal out of it ever since.

Here's what happened. Last September I was all excited about French Club, because French is my second-favorite class, after art. I went to a few meetings and then I found out that French Club wasn't about speaking French, watching French movies, and eating French snacks like baguettes and Brie cheese. I found out that the whole purpose of the club was to get ready for a big summer trip to Paris.

Everyone in the club goes.

That's what French Club is really all about.

When I told Nana, she said, "France? How much is *that* going to cost?"

I waved the trip information flyer Madame Girard had sent home, but Nana acted like she didn't see it. "Um, we sell candy bars and do car washes and stuff to pay for it?"

Nana said, "I hope you're not going to start pestering everyone to buy candy bars."

I knew right then that I wasn't going to Paris. So there was no more point in going to French Club.

That should have been the end of my French Club problem, but instead it was the start. Mr. Burns noticed I wasn't going to French Club anymore. He asked why I stopped going, and I told him. Now I swear he won't let it go.

At least as of Christmas I have a passport, so if I ever have a chance to go to France, I'll be prepared. It was literally the only thing I put on my wish list. Nana was annoyed, but she got me one. I figure if I have a passport, it must mean I'm going to go somewhere, someday, besides the Wegmans grocery store in Parsippany.

I tell Mr. Burns, "No, I didn't ask her again about the French Club trip."

"Why not?"

"Because it wouldn't make a difference. She never changes her mind about anything like that."

"Did you tell her that fundraising pays for most of the trip, and there are plenty of chaperones?"

I shake my head.

Mr. Burns scribbles something. "I think it would be a good thing if you asked your nana about this trip just once more. If she has any questions, she can call me and I'll get them answered. It's not too late yet, but it's going to be too late soon. Anything else going on? No? Head on back to class, then. Don't forget to ask your grandmother, okay? I'm going to be checking in with her."

I am not getting out of this.

CHAPTER 2

DINNER THAT NIGHT IS what we usually have on Thursday: quiche. Nana likes to use up the leftovers before Friday, when she does the grocery shopping. I poke at it. I don't mind quiche, but it looks like Nana put the leftover squash in it.

Nana is telling me about one of her patients that day, some guy who always lies about flossing and then gets surprised when his gums bleed.

"Does he really think we can't tell he's lying?" my grandmother demands, slicing into a piece of tomato like it's a stretch of swollen gum tissue.

Nana works as a dental hygienist and people who fib about their dental hygiene habits drive her wild.

"I know, it's so wack," I say. Personally, I love to floss. I love the way my teeth feel after I'm done.

I look around our dining nook. It's not a separate room, just one end of our corridor kitchen where Nana managed to cram in a little table that's just big enough for three people, because one of its sides is against the wall. If we have more than three people eating, one of them has to sit in the rocking chair with a plate. Not like that happens very often.

"Anything interesting happen to you today?" Nana asks. She likes us to chat a little at dinner, instead of just sitting there like lumps listening to the news on NPR.

I remember Mr. Burns and say, "Oh, Nana," before I remember that I didn't want to bring that whole thing up.

"Yes?" she prompts me.

"Mr. Burns wanted me to ask you about the French Club trip again." I say it in a small voice, because I know Nana isn't going to like this.

"No," Nana says.

"He wanted me to tell you—"

"No."

I know better than to say anything else, but Nana goes right on anyway like I'd tried to argue.

"You are twelve years old. I think you can hold off on a trip to Europe until high school at least." She says "Europe" like it's the most ridiculous place on the planet. Which is totally bizarre. Nana's dad was from Italy and my poppy's parents came from Poland. I bet if Poppy were here, he'd have something to say about Europe being a totally normal place to visit.

"I've already got my passport," I hear myself say.

"I knew that's why you wanted it," Nana snaps.

She's always really tired on Thursday nights.

I wish I had never mentioned it.

It's time to clear away. I stack the plates with a clatter I know will annoy Nana. And then I play this game I invented, which involves tossing the cutlery into the sink from the entrance to the kitchen. It's harder than it seems, but the knives are easier than the forks.

"Franny!" Nana raises her voice. "Stop that and take the garbage downstairs for me."

I ignore her.

Here's the thing: maybe I am only twelve, but people from my school go everywhere.

Ruben goes to the Philippines every summer to see his grandparents. For, like, a whole month. Camp Cebu, he calls it, after the island where his grandparents live.

Lucy has been all kinds of places. She was born in London, so she got a head start right there. And besides that, she's been all over Europe, to Israel, Thailand, and Singapore. She even went to Kenya on safari.

Well, I want to go somewhere too.

"Can you *please* deal with that garbage?" Nana says.

I hate taking the garbage out. We live in an apartment over a coffee shop downtown. We have to carry our garbage down the stairs and then out the door while people who are waiting for their coffee look at us. It's so embarrassing. And then we carry it around behind the building to the dumpster out back and hope that the bag doesn't leak or smear grease everywhere.

So I ignore Nana. I open the dishwasher and start a new game, which involves trying to drop knives and forks straight into the cutlery basket. Mostly they bounce out into the bottom of the dishwasher and onto the floor. I'm going to pick them up, and they're getting washed anyway, so who cares? It's just to see what happens. Just for fun. If you ask me, we could use a little more of that around here.

"I don't have the energy for this." Without looking at me, Nana yanks the garbage bag out of the can and walks past me to our door. She doesn't slam the door, but she definitely closes it louder than usual.

Once Nana has gone out, there's no reason to keep being a pain, so I stop messing around and finish loading the dishwasher. I wipe off the counter and the table and shove the chairs in. Then I go off to my bedroom.

I feel better there. My room is a lot smaller than Nana's, but Nana's looks out on Valley Road, which means she has a beautiful view of the bank across the street, the cars waiting at the traffic light, and the train station parking lot. It's fine if you like that whole Edward Hopper vibe, but I see enough of that going back and forth to school every day. I only have my one window, but it looks out over people's backyards. I can watch them filling bird feeders, jumping on trampolines, checking food in barbecues . . . It looks fun. My whole life, I don't think I've lived anywhere with a yard. Not that I remember.

I get my journal off my bureau and sit down on the futon. That's what I sleep on, because I guess when I first came to live with Nana I wasn't used to beds. She'd always find me on the floor in the morning and worry because it was hard and cold, and the futon was our compromise.

"Journal" sounds a lot more grown-up than "diary." Sometimes I do use it to write about what happened to me, but mostly I use it to record the lists of Things Currently Worrying Franny Petroski. If you look back through the lists, they almost make up a journal, in a different kind of way.

Once, one of my school counselors suggested I keep a gratitude journal and every day write down five things I felt grateful for. I got tired of that pretty fast.

It's not that I don't feel grateful.

It's just that I get *told* to feel grateful a lot.

So instead of writing down things I was grateful for, I started writing down the things that worried me. I like that better. It helps me keep track. Also, when I look back through my lists, I can see how many things fixed themselves. Or time fixed them. For example, from my past lists:

What camp I'm going to this summer
(Camp on the Lake, same as always.)

Sitting next to Mark Behrend in Language Arts

(That was horrible, but then Mark Behrend moved away and fixed that problem for me.)

Math test

(Last week. I didn't do very well, but at least that worry ended fast.)

I think over my day and then write down a few things.

Executive skills

French Club trip

I yawn and rub my nose. Then I write down one more:

Mom

I stare at the word.

Uh, where did *that* come from?

I don't think about my mom.

She never thinks about *us*. Yeah, so I don't think about her, either.

I grab my good gum eraser, the one I usually only use for drawing, and erase the word until no one would know it was ever there. Then to make sure, I write over the spot where it was.

Ruben's fish

But I just wrote that down to have something there. I don't worry about Ruben's fish. I know Dr. Yao takes tender care of even the smallest snail in that tank.

I growl, rip the whole page out, and scrunch it. I drop it in my wastebasket.

Ugh! Usually when I do my list, I feel better, like I've transferred all my worry out of my brain and into the notebook and left it there. Not tonight.

I smack the notebook back on top of my bureau and leave my room to see what Nana's doing.

No Nana. She's not anywhere in the apartment.

Huh.

That's weird.

Maybe she walked up to the grocery store for something.

It's only a few blocks from here, but I'm pretty sure she would have said something.

Maybe she stopped to get us hot chocolate?

She does that sometimes, before Java Dream, the coffee shop downstairs, closes up. It would be a weird thing for her to do tonight, though. Nana doesn't believe in rewarding what she calls "poor choices," and I know she was mad about the way I loaded the dishwasher. But I can't think of anywhere else she could be.

I grab my key and go downstairs. The moment I push open our outside door, I know something is wrong. The guys from Java Dream are out on the sidewalk, and there's a small knot of people standing around.

"She took a face-plant," I hear someone say.

"Why doesn't anyone ever salt these sidewalks along here?" a lady with a puffy coat and beat-up briefcase says. "Whose responsibility is it?"

I see two crunched white takeaway cups from the coffee shop abandoned on the sidewalk, and a big light brown pool of liquid has spread all the way across the cement.

"Nana?" I say.

Then I shout. "Nana! Nana!"

I shove my way through the adults to where Nana is sitting on the ground. She is holding her nose and her whole face is bloody. But what's worse is the way she's sitting. One leg under her, the other at a weird angle in front. And the way she looks—scared.

"Oh, Franny," she says. "I decided to get us some hot chocolate, but then somehow I slipped—what a stupid old fool I am!"

She sounds even more scared than she looks. That does it for me. I'm instantly terrified. My insides twist, and bitter-tasting stomach juices slosh up into my mouth.

I kneel down by her. Red lights start flashing across everyone's faces, and an ambulance draws up to the curb.

CHAPTER 3

I HATE THE SMELL OF hospitals. I also hate the bright lights and the weird buzzing noises coming from so many different things. I'm also pretty sure I hate this doctor talking to Nana, even though I know Nana herself would not approve. If she were paying attention to me, she'd be saying, "Now, he's just trying to help."

"Okay—Antonella? Can I call you that?"

No one calls Nana "Antonella." It's always "Andi." But she doesn't bother telling this doctor that.

"Antonella, what we have here is a tibial plateau fracture. We see these most commonly with auto accidents. But a good solid fall onto a hard surface will do it too, like what happened to you."

I can just see the little dark line running through Nana's bone.

Nana squints at the image on the computer. She makes a note on the pad of paper someone in the ER lent her. It took a while for them to find some paper for her. I've tried telling her everyone uses their phones now.

"You've been very lucky, young lady!" the doctor goes on.

Seriously? I say in my head. The doctor gives me a startled look, and I realize too late that I said it out loud. I have a bad habit of doing that sometimes.

Nana bunches her eyebrows together and throws me a look that means, *Frances! Behave yourself.* Nana says you're allowed to think whatever you want, but it's a good idea to keep some of those thoughts to yourself.

"We're going to do a quick surgery and get some screws in your leg here and here." The doctor's pen taps different places on the screen. He stands back and tilts his head to one side. "Then you should be good to go. We'll keep you here overnight and get that surgery done as early as we can tomorrow." The doctor scratches his beard. He sounds thoughtful as he adds, "The surgery should be straightforward. The rehab is what's complicated in these cases."

"What does that involve." I can tell how tired Nana is because her questions don't have question marks at the ends anymore. They just sound like flat sentences.

"We're talking eight weeks with the leg immobilized and fully extended. Then I'd say four weeks in a hinged brace. Totally NWB, of course—"

"What's that mean."

The doctor smiles apologetically. "'Non-weight bearing.' Sorry. Then we'll start serious physical therapy, probably something like three times a week. Eventually you'll be able to resume functional activities like walking, stair climbing, swimming, driving—of course, all that after your leg heals and gets stronger and you've done enough PT."

I think all this over. I ask, "What if you live in a second-floor apartment?"

The doctor pauses, then gives us a bright smile. "Do you have an elevator?"

Nana closes her eyes and takes a deep, patient breath.

"WHAT ARE WE GOING to do, Nana?" I ask. We're in another stale little room, waiting for someone to do something—I'm not sure what. It seems like hospitals are bursts of activity and long sessions of sitting around waiting for something to happen. There's one of those weird hospital hums in the air and everything around us looks a little grimy and tired, though it's obviously supposed to be mega clean.

Nana blinks. Her blinks are getting longer and longer. She gives her head a little shake. "Ugh, this pain med is knocking me out. Honeybee, ask the nurse whether you can use the phone and call Gracie. She can come and pick you up. I don't want you staying overnight in the hospital. It's no place for a kid, and anyway, I'm not sure where you'd sleep."

"*Not* Aunt Gravy!" I know I shouldn't be moaning, but I can't help it.

Aunt Gravy and Nana worked together at Dr. Morgenstern's

practice until Aunt Gravy retired last year. They're besties. They talk on the phone every day. I call her Aunt Gravy because for some weird reason her house, clothes, and hair always smell like gravy. Even Nana admits it. Aunt Gravy also has bristles on her chin and a constant apologetic smile, and she can never remember that I'm a vegetarian.

Put it this way: Nana is super lit compared to Aunt Gravy.

"Stop calling her Gravy. You're going to let it slip in front of her sometime and it's going to hurt her feelings. And quit being a pain. It's just for one night."

How does Nana know that? What if something happens during the operation?

What if she has to stay extra long at the hospital?

Will I have to stay longer with Aunt Gravy?

Or will Aunt Gravy just call Social Services and tell them to come and get me?

I imagine one of those conversations with adults talking across me like I can't hear them.

"The grandmother, who normally takes care of her, is currently incapacitated—"

That's the kind of thing they say.

"No one knows where the mother is—"

"The father is unknown, not in the picture—"

That's the way some people talk. Lawyers, social workers, judges, people like that. Don't get me wrong—there are some nice ones. But for some reason you only remember the ones who talk like that about your family right in front of you. Like it's so broken it could never be right.

"Deep breaths. Deep breaths." Nana puts her hand on my back. "Let me think for a moment."

She closes her eyes. She looks so tired, I hate her for a moment. Why does she have to be so . . . old? Why can't she be younger, like everyone else's parents?

Then I see how worried she is, on top of everything else, and I hate myself, too, for being so mean. It's not her fault she's ancient.

I carefully slide the notepad off her lap and tear a few sheets from the back so I don't mess up all of Nana's notes. Then I take the pen out of her fingers. She doesn't twitch. I think she may have fallen asleep.

I write down *Things Currently Worrying Franny Petroski* across the top and get writing.

> What if something happens to Nana during the operation?
>
> What if Nana has to stay longer at the hospital?
>
> How are we going to get home from the hospital when Nana's car is back at the apartment?
>
> How can Nana fit into a taxi if she can't bend her knee?

Where are we going to live now?
How will we get groceries?
How will Nana get to work?
How can Nana work if she can't stand?
How will Nana use the toilet?
How will Nana take a shower?
Where will I stay tonight?

The first page is already filled up and I've barely gotten started. I flip to the next and keep writing.

"The Yaos," Nana says.

I jump, and the pen flies out of my fingers and rattles across the floor. I get up to grab it. "Ruben's parents? What about them, Nana?"

"Maybe you could stay with the Yaos tonight," Nana says. "They're good people. Franny, find a nurse or someone and ask if we can use a phone before it gets any later. I think these pain meds are affecting my speech centers, and I don't want to be slurring when I talk to them."

～⌒～

THAT NIGHT, RUBEN AND I have a sleepover down in the Yaos' basement, like old times.

Even though it's still Thursday night, Ruben's parents are treating it like it's a weekend. Which is fun but also strange. I already know I don't have to go to school tomorrow, because I'm going to the hospital to wait until Nana is out of surgery.

And Dr. Yao said that Ruben can sleep in and go to school late. "You can be tardy for once," she said.

Ruben and I used to have sleepovers a lot when we were little. A few years ago they stopped, and we didn't know why, until Ruben's big sister, Reyna, finally told us it was because Ruben and I are members of the opposite sex. It was no longer "appropriate," the adults had decided. Which was pretty stupid, because Ruben and I are like brother and sister. But—adults. You know. Did they listen? No way.

Anyway, our sleeping bags are downstairs in the Yaos' basement. Dr. Yao lets us eat snacks and watch one episode of *The Mandalorian* before it's lights-out.

Reyna is with us. I think she was supposed to chaperone or something, but she just ignored us and played games on her phone until she curled up on the sofa and fell asleep. We can tell she's asleep because she snores. Reyna has allergies.

In our sleeping bags, it's comfy on the carpeted floor.

I'm almost asleep when Ruben speaks up. "Do you think it's weird your nana doesn't have any family who could help out?"

From the way he says it, I know he's echoing something he heard his mom or dad say.

Ruben has seven aunts and uncles and eighteen cousins. True story. He sees the Filipino cousins every summer, and the American cousins every Christmas. Reyna and Ruben get more Christmas presents than you could probably imagine.

(Just in case you were wondering, Nana's rule at Christmas is three presents. She says that's plenty.)

But here's the difference between Ruben and so many other people. He never says stuff to be mean. So even though the question stings a little, it's not a big hurt—more like a paper cut.

"Well, my great-grandparents are dead, and Nana's brother died in a car accident when he was pretty young. There's my uncle Gabe, but he lives in Wisconsin."

I can feel Ruben thinking. Then he says, "How about your mom? Does anyone ever hear from her?"

I bet you anything he heard one of his parents ask that, too.

Ruben knows I don't like to talk about my mom.

He's breaking one of our rules.

"Uh, no, Rubes. We don't." I say it like this is kind of a weird thing to be talking about. That usually works to end these conversations. Except tonight, for some reason, I add, "Nana always says Mom had some stuff to work out."

"But how long will it take for her to work it out?"

My act fails. "Ruben, I don't know and I don't care!"

Reyna gives a snort and turns over on the sofa.

"I find that difficult to believe," Ruben observes, "because she's your mom."

"Yeah? Well, Nana had to take care of me because Mom didn't. And she never calls or writes, so forget her."

"She's not dead, right?"

My heart speeds up. But I make myself sigh, like this is kind of boring. "Rubes, I told you I just made that up."

When I was in kindergarten for the second time, I told everyone my mom was dead and that was why I lived with my grandmother. When the teacher found out I was lying, it was a big old mess. But sometimes I wish I could lie about it again. Because one thing about telling people your mom is dead, they don't usually ask anything else after that.

Inside my sleeping bag, I cross my fingers and hope Ruben is done with his questions for tonight.

My wish comes true. Ruben yawns. "I've got to get some sleep."

"I do too," I say. But then I just lie there staring up at the ceiling.

BEFORE NANA AND ME there was Mom and me. Sometimes there were other people around, and I think I remember that some of them were cool, but we never stayed anywhere for long, Nana says. So mostly it was just Mom and me.

Then I came to live with Nana, and now it's Nana and me. There's no one else in our family, except for Uncle Gabe. He and Nana don't get along. I'm not sure I've ever met him.

One thing I know from living with Mom is that when things are going okay, one person is enough. But when something bad happens, one person is not always enough. At those times, you need more than one person in your life.

But what if you don't have more than one person and something bad happens? What do you do?

What happens to you then?

CHAPTER 4

I CAN'T TELL YOU HOW grateful I am," Nana says for the fifth or sixth time this half hour.

"It's no trouble," Dr. Yao reassures her.

Dr. Yao doesn't sound annoyed, but she is starting to sound like someone keeping her patience. Like she wishes Nana would finish up and stop thanking her already.

It's early Monday morning and we're in Dr. Yao's big old Subaru, driving uptown along Valley Road toward a house that we might be able to rent.

At first Nana said we would go stay with Aunt Gravy for a few days after the surgery. That would give us some time to figure out where we could live while Nana's knee got better.

That's what Nana said, anyway. I have an idea she was secretly hoping we could just stay with Aunt Gravy. Luckily (as far as I'm concerned) that didn't work out. It turned out that even though Aunt Gravy's yard had room for a temporary ramp to her kitchen door, that door was too narrow for Nana's wheelchair to get through.

"*Ironside* makes it look so easy," Aunt Gravy said. She

was panting from the effort of getting Nana up and down the ramp.

Ironside is this old show on the oldies station about a detective in a wheelchair. The show isn't at all realistic. I know that now. I mean, if you were a criminal and wanted to stop Ironside from catching you, all you would have to do is hide out on the second floor of a house with stairs and no elevator. How hard is that to figure out?!

When the Yaos found out Aunt Gravy's house wouldn't work for Nana and me, they said that of course we were welcome to stay with them. Nana told me that they probably didn't mean that. They were just saying it to be kind. But we didn't have a lot of other options, unless we wanted to live in one of those motels out on Route 46, the kind where all the rooms are strung out in a single row along the parking lot. And that's counting on Nana's wheelchair fitting through the doors.

Even getting in and out of the Yaos" house isn't easy. It's not just that Nana's in the wheelchair; it's that her leg is stuck out totally straight in front of her. It can't bend. And it won't be bending for the next two months. So not only does her wheelchair need to fit through doors, there has to be extra room for her stuck-out leg.

And don't get me started on Nana using the bathroom. That's a whole other thing that I do not care to describe.

Which is why when Dr. Yao told us this morning about some

friends of friends who were renting a wheelchair-equipped house for a few months, Nana jumped at the chance to look at it.

"The man who lived there, Mr. Tan, has kidney cancer that metastasized to his liver, so he can't walk anymore," Dr. Yao told us. "That's why the house is fitted out for a wheelchair. And now his health has gotten worse again, and he's staying with his daughter. Ay sus! The house is just sitting empty while the family figures out what to do. They're willing to give you a big break on the rent just to make sure there's someone living there."

Nana nods. "Things happen in empty houses."

Dr. Yao snaps on her turn signal and pulls next to the curb. Dr. Yao is one of those grown-ups who drives the speed limit through our town no matter how many cars line up behind her on the road. They're like a bunch of angry bees zooming by now as we get out.

The house is small and square, one story. It's made out of a dull yellow brick the exact color of dental plaque. (Nana brings home lots of informational pamphlets, which is how I know.) So maybe this is destiny. On one side of the front door, a big picture window bulges out like a weird eye, and on the other side of the door a string of little rectangular windows runs along under the roof. From the look of the ragged bushes in front, it looks like the deer find them delicious.

But I can see Nana is checking out one thing only: the ramp

leading from the walkway to the house's front stoop. Dr. Yao pushes Nana up the ramp to the stoop, and there Nana takes over. She wheels herself back and forth, turns to face the door, turns away again—and that's all just to get the key in the lock!

Her lips are moving. I'm pretty sure she's swearing in Italian. She learned all these curse words from her dad and uses them when she doesn't want to offend people.

Now Nana's finally gotten the house open and she disappears inside calling, "Come and take a look!"

I climb the steps instead of using the ramp.

I swear I'm never taking my knees for granted again.

There's no front hallway, like we have in our apartment. We just step into the big main room. There's a mat by the door with some abandoned old shoes scattered across it. I'm pretty sure I know what Mr. Tan's feet smell like now. The carpet was cream once, but now it's gray and kind of matted down. The sofa and recliner are both covered in brown prickly cloth. The pictures on the walls are of things like kittens and covered bridges.

On the kitchen side of this room, the linoleum has been torn up in a few spots and mended with duct tape. I think the kitchen counters were light green once, but the sun has faded them to something more like greenish white.

"The last avocado kitchen appliances in existence," Nana mutters.

But without any walls, the kitchen is big and open. Nana can move around in there pretty easily. The kitchen table is already shoved against one wall, and the most important cooking stuff is all in the drawers and the bottom cabinets.

Nana takes off down the hall to inspect the bedrooms and the bathroom. They're nothing special, except that the bathroom has been fitted out for a person in a wheelchair. That's a relief! Nana will be able to use the toilet and shower by herself.

"The basement is through that door," Dr. Yao says. "There's another bedroom and bathroom down there, and the washer and dryer. If you want, we can go back out and go down through the garage so you can have a look. Assuming the wheelchair fits through the basement door."

"Oh, I think Franny can do that for us. Honeybee, go down and take a look around. Check out the washer and dryer. You're going to be the one on laundry duty for a while."

The washer and dryer have rust stains, but both spring to life when I twiddle their knobs and push the right buttons.

I look around the rest of the basement. It's dirty and gloomy and smells closed up, but there's plenty of space. Dusty boxes and all kinds of junk are stacked neatly around the walls.

I stick my head into the basement bedroom. It's darker than the bedrooms upstairs because its windows are gray with cobwebs. On the bed is a white bedspread covered with bumps that make a pattern. I run my hand over the loops, and all of a sudden its name comes to me. It's a candlewick bedspread.

A really strong memory of Mom pops into my head.

We were in a room with a bedspread like this and I was afraid of it, for some dumb reason. Well, I must have been super little. Mom took my hand in hers and ran it over the loops, and then I laughed, because they tickled. Mom laughed too. She had short, raggedy nails, the kind you get when you bite them off, and her hair hung down almost to the bed. Her hair was the color of caramels. I would twirl it around my hand when I was falling asleep in her lap.

Even though I know people are waiting for me, I stay there awhile, rubbing the bedspread with both hands.

Nana and Dr. Yao are talking in the hallway when I come back upstairs.

"They're just happy to have someone living in the house, and they know it's not in the greatest shape, so a break in the rent seems fair."

"You're not fooling me, Adela. I'd bet anything you put in a word with them."

"I may have said something, but it's no big deal, honestly. It's a win-win for everyone."

I tell them, "The washer and dryer work."

"Great." Nana turns back to Dr. Yao. "Is this afternoon too early to move in?"

I look at Nana. We were supposed to look at a first-floor apartment today too. I bet it's newer and cleaner and doesn't have any candlewick bedspreads. Then I feel a sudden surge of worry. "Are we giving up *our* apartment?"

"No, silly girl. That's the point. We'll be able to pay the rent on both. This place is furnished. All we need are a few suitcases of clothes and a trip to the grocery store, and we can move right in."

That's a relief. I can't wait for things to go back to normal, and for the list of Things Currently Worrying Franny Petroski to shrink down to a normal size.

CHAPTER 5

WHEN I GET HOME from Homework Club on Tuesday, Nana is inching her way down the front ramp with one hand firmly on the wheelchair brake. Nana doesn't like going fast at the best of times, and I think she has a vision of her wheelchair gathering speed and dumping her out onto the sidewalk. Aunt Gravy is waiting at the bottom of the ramp looking stressed, like she usually does, and apologizing for being late, like she always is. "I had to walk Chester, and he just would not hurry up today."

Chester is Aunt Gravy's ancient dachshund.

Nana calls, "Franny! I forgot I have a follow-up appointment at the doctor's. But it won't be long. Finish your homework and turn the oven on to 425° at five o'clock, okay?"

"Okay. What are we having for dinner?"

"Frozen dinners." Nana sounds short, but I'm pretty sure she's annoyed at Aunt Gravy for being late. Nana hates being late for anything.

Yay. I love frozen dinners. We never get to have them usually. It's nice to be alone in the house. It's been days since I was alone. I eat an apple and some cookies, then I head off to the bathroom for a pit stop.

Something weird happens when I flush.

The sound is wrong. There's not the reassuring glug of the water going down the pipe. The toilet bowl is filling up instead of emptying.

That doesn't seem good.

I'm not sure what's going on. You never think about a toilet when it's working the way it's supposed to. I try flushing it again.

The water does not glug. Instead it starts rising faster. It's going up, up, up, over the rim onto the bathroom floor while I stare at it in horror.

"No!" I shout, like the toilet can hear me and cares what I think. "No, no, no!"

The toilet paper I just used settles cozily over my sneaker and I shake it off into a corner and look around wildly. The bathroom floor is totally wet. The water starts pouring out into the hall. It splashes against the opposite wall and start spreading out, toward the carpet in the living room, and our bedrooms.

What do I do?!

Towels! I need towels! Luckily the linen closet is right there in the hall and there are plenty of towels stacked up, even if they are old and thin. I dam up the water in the bathroom by piling the towels across the doorway and then throw a few over the mess in the hallway. It's working right now, but it won't for much longer. The towels are already getting wet.

I run down to the kitchen and try the old-fashioned phone hung on the wall. To my vast relief there's a dial tone. I punch in Ruben's phone number as fast as I can.

Ruben answers the way he's supposed to. "Yao residence."

"It's Franny! Listen, do you know how to stop a toilet from flooding?"

"What?"

"Flooding!" I shout. "I flushed it and now water's running all over the floor! Do you know how to make it stop?"

I pull the phone cord tight so I can see around the corner into the hall. The towel dam is still holding, but the towels are starting to look soaked. I'm in a panic. In another moment, I'm going to pee my own pants from anxiety, just like back in second grade with Mrs. Dixon.

"Okay, first you have to turn off the water. Go down to the bathroom and I'll talk you through that."

I start walking toward the bathroom and just in time I remember this phone has a cord. I probably would have yanked it out of the wall otherwise. "Rubes, this phone is in the kitchen and I can't take it with me. You're going to have to walk me through this. I'll do one thing at a time and then I'll come back for you to tell me what to do next. You'll have to hold on the line. Okay?"

"Really? Cool. Old-fashioned tech, huh?" Ruben has a fascination with old-fashioned tech. "We can do that."

"Don't hang up, Ruben!"

"I won't hang up. So, first you need to find the pipe going from the toilet to the wall—"

JUST IN CASE YOU ever have to unclog a toilet, this is what you do.

First you find the valve on the pipe running from the toilet into the floor. It looks like a handle. You have to turn that valve until the water stops running. You'll know the water has stopped running because everything will go quiet.

Then you have to find a plunger, which you'll know when you see it. And judging from where Mr. Tan keeps his, right by the toilet, I think maybe he used it a lot. His has a wooden handle with a half circle of red rubber on one end. You fit the rubber part over the bottom of the toilet and push it up and down until the toilet unclogs and the water drains out.

"It creates a vacuum. Which is pretty cool, huh?" Ruben loves science.

Then you can turn the water back on. Once the bowl has filled itself again, you flush it one more time to make sure the clog has cleared.

And then you get to wipe up all the water on the bathroom floor and in the hall, because you can't just leave it like that.

And you take all the towels you used to stop the flood and start washing them, because they're all dirty. (Hint: this may take more than one load. More like two or three.)

Then you need to find some kind of cleaning stuff, a bucket, and a mop, and mop the bathroom and hallway.

"Because, you know, the water has pee in it," Ruben explains.

"I *know*, Ruben!"

"Okay, geez! I'm just trying to help."

When I come up from taking the last armful of towels down to the laundry room, Nana and Aunt Gravy are in the living room. Nana doesn't look too happy. She starts scolding me right away. "Why isn't the oven on? Dinner's going to be late now, and I asked your aunt Gracie to stay."

I swear Aunt Gracie is the only person I know who would get excited about staying for a TV dinner.

"I can turn it on." Aunt Gracie goes into the kitchen. "How are you feeling, Andi? Is your leg still hurting?"

"Yes," my nana raps out. She still isn't done with me. "Did you get your homework done at least?"

I think about telling Nana about my afternoon, and then stop. I don't feel like describing the toilet disaster with Aunt Gracie there. It was embarrassing enough to live through without having to describe it afterward.

So I just say, "Most of it."

"Then set the table and go finish your homework before

dinner. I shouldn't have to remind you to get your work done, Franny. Come on, you're in sixth grade now."

I think of the massive stack of books and papers on the desk in my room. I have a desk because I got the master bedroom. Nana couldn't stay in there because the entrance didn't work with her leg in extension. "Nana? Do you think you could help me with the math?"

Nana hates helping with my math, because she learned how to do it a totally different way and Mr. Winkler doesn't like the way she solves the problems. "Why didn't you get help with that at Homework Club?"

"Because I needed help with my ELA essay instead," I mutter. Sometimes it feels like I need help with everything that has to do with school. Aside from art and French.

"Oh. Well, bring it out here, and Gracie and I will do the best we can. You know I can't get into your bedroom with my leg like this."

Aunt Gracie comes back into sight, sniffing. "Anyway, it smells nice and clean in here. Like someone's been mopping with Pine-Sol."

I make a quick getaway to find my homework.

NANA HAS THIS WEIRD old saying she brings out sometimes: "It never rains but it pours."

For ages she wouldn't tell me what it meant, because she

likes me to figure things out for myself and she says I'm perfectly capable. But finally she took pity on me. "It means that for whatever reason bad things seem to happen in bunches," she said.

Well, that was simple, and I wondered why Nana hadn't just said that to start with.

I'm at my locker after school on Wednesday, trying to remember all the books I need while also getting in the right headspace for Studio Club.

When I'm getting ready for Studio Club or art class, I get into a different part of my head. That sounds weird. All I mean is a different part of my brain turns on—a part that doesn't have anything to do with spelling or facts or math formulas. And just in case you think I'm making all this up, Miss Midori says it's a "well-recognized phenomena." There's a book, *Drawing on the Right Side of the Brain*, about it. I did a book report on it last fall and it was the first time I got an A on a book report. Nana was so happy, she put it up on the fridge. It's still there, back in our apartment.

That part of my brain is where I feel the most comfortable. Where I usually know what to do next and I've got plenty of ideas. Where I get to feel smart, like Ruben and Lucy do all the time. I wish I got to spend more time in that part and less time in the part that needs to know how to divide fractions and remember what day of the week it is.

Lucy comes up beside me. "Hey, do you have a second?"

"You want to walk down to Studio Club together?"

Lucy and I are both in Studio Club. We became friends in art class back in elementary school, because we both love art so much. We do different stuff, though. Lucy likes ceramics. Her mom throws pots and Lucy grew up messing around with clay. No Play-Doh in Lucy's house. And she doesn't think much of my salt dough, either, but nobody's perfect.

"I'm not going today." Lucy sounds kind of funny. Like her words are coming out under pressure.

I sigh to myself and come out from my art space into the space where I have to talk to people.

We go outside and sit on the bench in the memorial garden. The garden is for a middle-school girl who died a long time ago really suddenly. To be honest it's not my favorite place at school, even though I know it was a nice thing for the girl's family to do for her. It always makes me think about how old Nana is and about the whole death thing. Which isn't my favorite subject to dwell on. It's another thing that comes up pretty frequently on the lists of Things Currently Worrying Franny Petroski. We sit for a moment, watching all the kids we know scrambling to get on their buses while Mr. Winkler shouts for them to stop running.

"Something *bad* has happened," Lucy says. "Do you remember when Dad had to move to London last fall?"

"Sure." I remember Lucy said that her dad's company was

opening a new London office and needed him there to oversee operations for a while. I also remember feeling super envious because they'd be going to London for Christmas. I want to go to London, mostly because of all of Lucy's stories about it. I want to go to the Victoria and Albert Museum, which Lucy has described as the world's biggest attic full of the best junk ever.

"Do you remember that Mum said something then about how it was too much time for the family to be apart? And maybe we should all move to London for a while?"

"I remember." I study the side of Lucy's face. Her red hair hangs down straight to her shoulders from under her knit hat, and her skin is dusted with freckles the way Nana sometimes dusts sugar cookies with cinnamon.

Lucy sniffs and swipes her nose with her mitten. "Well, Mum said that *once* and didn't say anything more about it. And then she mentioned it again when we were in London for the holidays and asked what we thought? And then nothing more again! And then—last night—Mum said she had decided it was a *good idea*!"

If you try to write out the way Lucy sounds when she talks, you have to use a lot of question marks, exclamation points, and italics. It's just the way she is.

I blink. "You mean you're . . . moving?"

"It's not permanent." Then Lucy's forehead crinkles up. "I *hope*. But we're supposed to go week after *next*! And we'll be

47

there the whole spring semester, and probably the summer, too! Mum's already recruited everyone she knows back home to help us find school places." Aside from an English accent and the fact that she calls her mom "Mum," cool things "brilliant," and bad things "rancid," Lucy is as New Jersey as the rest of us in our middle school and it's weird to hear her call London "home," even if she was born there. "*And*—we're living with my gran."

Lucy's gran is a total stiff. Way worse than Nana, judging from Lucy's stories.

"I'm so *mad*! I said, 'You can't just *spring* this on us!' And Mum said, 'Now, darling'"—Lucy hates it when her mother calls her "darling"—"'we did talk about it, and you said it was fine.' I'm not speaking to her right now! And Ned and Finn aren't happy either!"

Ned is Lucy's older brother, Finn is her younger one.

I can't think of what to say next.

I get how Lucy feels, because London is no big deal for her and she doesn't like staying in her gran's house, let alone living there.

But—I also know I would love to do what she's going to do.

Once, Lucy and I talked about this idea for a graphic novel set in a world where kids figure out how to switch places with each other. They could find out what it's like to be in someone else's skin. Like *Freaky Friday*, only our kids could do it on purpose, whenever they wanted. This is one of those times when for sure I would switch places with Lucy if I had the chance. Even though I know I wouldn't feel all that comfortable in Lucy's family, where, to put it the way Nana does, expectations are high. Where table manners are important, and the kids all take piano lessons whether they like the piano or not, and there had better be good grades on the report cards. I don't think I would fit in there very well.

"I'm going to miss you, Lulz," I say at last.

"I'm going to miss *you*!" Lucy bursts out. "And you can't even text, so I guess we're just going to have to *email* each other all the time until I'm back." She sniffs again. "I'd say you should come visit, but would your nana let you?"

That question just adds to my general misery.

If Nana won't let me go to Europe with a big group and a bunch of chaperones, she's not going to let me go on my own, for sure.

Even if things were totally normal in our house. Which they aren't.

I just say, "I couldn't leave Nana right now, in a wheelchair and everything."

"That's what I thought." For once there's no question mark or exclamation point in what Lucy says.

CHAPTER 6

IN THE ART ROOM, everyone is already working hard on their projects. There's a low-level happy hum of everyone being busy and productive, and some jazz music playing. Miss Midori loves jazz, like I do. There aren't very many kids in my grade who listen to it. The first time Miss Midori put on WBGO (which is this great music station out of Newark), some kids asked what kind of music it was. Miss Midori's jazz fandom was one of the first things that made me like her. Wynton Marsalis is on right now.

In Studio Club, we get to work on whatever we want.

If you want to work on your project for art class, you can do that.

If you want to work on something for yourself, you can do that.

If you want to work on pieces to show at the Studio Club Open House, which is coming up in March, cool. If you don't, cool.

If you want to just sit around on your stool and enjoy the art room atmosphere, you can do that, or so Miss Midori always says.

Art was the first class I was ever good in. Where a teacher was impressed by something I did. That didn't happen to me in any other class for a long time. I like drawing and painting. I like making prints and doing ceramics. I like papier-mâché. I like pretty much anything you can do in an art class, but lately what I do the most is what Miss Midori calls "exploring unusual materials."

Like that kite I found stuck in the bushes. That's the kind of thing I narrow in on. Too bad it's not here for me to work on. I took it home to the apartment the day Nana got hurt. But—it won't spoil. It'll be there when I'm ready for it.

Nana is not a fan of unusual materials. She says I hang on to all kinds of useless junk and that she had better not catch me climbing out of a dumpster again, the way she did once when she was driving home from work.

There was a hubcap in there I needed for our "life circle" project in art class.

What Nana doesn't know was the hubcap was a "found object" and there's a whole area of art dedicated to materials just like that! I've tried to explain it, but she just shakes her head.

Also, for what it's worth, my art teacher loved my life circle and put it in the display cabinet outside the school office.

Lately I've been doing more of that "enjoying the art room atmosphere" thing than I'd like. Keeping my hands busy, sure.

But not working on anything I'm really excited about. Nothing I would want at the Open House. (Not that art's about showing off what you can do. Miss Midori says it's more something you do for yourself.)

Maybe my nana doesn't mind rereading the same detective novels and tuning in to the same TV reruns again and again, but I think I need new stuff to keep my art wheels turning. New things to look at, new things to talk about.

Even something like being at the hospital can work. That wasn't super fun, but it was new. And today I have an idea. Not a coincidence if you ask me.

I go straight over to the bins in the corner and start looking through the recyclables that Miss Midori brings from home and takes away from the cafeteria, in spite of the strange looks she gets sometimes from people who see her rummaging around.

I start pulling things out and lining them up on the counter.

After a while Miss Midori comes over. Miss Midori's last name is Sato, but she says Miss Midori is fine. "Starting something new? Can I help?"

"I'm thinking about the hospital where I was with Nana," I tell her.

Like all my teachers, Miss Midori knows Nana hurt herself and was in the hospital. They all seemed to know in a day or two without me having to say anything. There's some kind of mysterious teacher telegraph in operation. Personally, I'm pretty sure it's located in the teachers' lounge. Lucy says it's probably at Finnegan's, the bar at the train station where a bunch of them like to go after work on Fridays.

Anyway, Miss Midori just nods. "Okay. What impressed you about that experience?"

"Well . . . everything there was kind of white but also kind of dirty?"

Miss Midori nods. "'Dingy,' maybe?" she offers.

"And the surfaces, like the floors and walls and tables and everything were hard and flat, and cold. So, I want to do something like that." I smooth out air with my hands, the way I sometimes do when I'm talking about a new project. "But also kind of *brittle*."

I show her my collection of milk cartons and jugs. They're all a little smelly and are going to need some washing before I get going. The insides of the milk cartons are a waxy white. The plastic milk jugs are kind of a see-through white that is also a little gray. They take on the color of what is inside them or behind them.

"Are you doing something flat this time?" Miss Midori asks.

She wants to know because I just went through a Judith Scott phase where I was wrapping a lot of stuff in cloth and plastic.

In case you don't know about Judith Scott, she was a total wow artist. She was deaf and had other impairments and couldn't talk, so she lived in group homes. They almost made her stop art classes because they didn't think she was getting anything out of them! True story! But then she took a fiber-art class and started making these amazing sculptures. She wrapped things. She wrapped a whole shopping cart once. And an armchair. Look her up and you'll see.

I wish I could do more stuff like hers, but . . . where could I wrap an armchair in our apartment?

Besides, Judith Scott already did it, and better than I would anyway. She was there first.

"I'm not sure," I tell Miss Midori. "I might be doing more of a box shape. Like something people could pick up and look inside?"

"Like Joseph Cornell? That sounds sick." Miss Midori can describe something as "sick" without coming off like some ridiculous grown-up trying too hard.

"I'll cut some shapes out of the milk cartons for the inside, and then maybe have these faces sort of floating against the back wall. I think I'm going to make the faces out of construction paper so they can be different colors? And they'll look kind of like that face from *Scream*." I drop my jaw and put on a horrified expression.

"The horror movie, or Edvard Munch's painting?"

I think for a moment. "Both. I mean, the faces in that movie and that painting look kind of alike."

"They do. It sounds like you have some interesting ideas. Let me know if I can help. And, Franny?"

I look up from the bins.

"Make sure you wash those jugs out well." Miss Midori laughs. "They really *stink*."

WHEN I GET HOME, the table is set. Nana can do that because of where the plates and glasses are kept. But there's no smell of cooking because I'm the one who has to put the frozen dinners in. The freezer is at the top of the fridge and Nana can't reach it. The oven isn't on either. Nana can't reach its controls from her wheelchair.

So I put the oven on first thing, even before I take off my coat. Nana is talking to someone on the phone. I can't tell whether she's mad at me, or just busy with her conversation. Then I take my backpack to my room and spread my homework out on the desk there and try to remember everything I have to do.

Then I go back to the kitchen and put the frozen dinners in and set the timer. I get us both glasses of water, get myself a glass of milk, and fix two salads from a box of romaine. I forget to put the salad dressing on the table and have to go back for that.

All the time Nana is saying, "Uh-huh. Uh-huh. No, she didn't mention that! No. Did it?"

I'm pretty sure she's not talking to Aunt Gravy, because when

Nana is talking to her, there are a lot more snorts and bursts of laughter. Maybe she's talking to the temp dental hygienist who's filling in for her at Dr. Morgenstern's.

I go downstairs to finish the laundry from yesterday. I have to switch one load of towels from the washer to the dryer. But before I do that, I have to fold the towels that are already in the dryer and put them on the card table next to the dryer. If you just dump them on the table, some of them will slither off onto the floor, and then they're dirty all over again. I've been learning that the hard way.

I put in the last load of dirty towels into the washer. Then the clean dry towels need to be put away.

The house is finally smelling like dinner, and I'm happy. My stomach is growling.

For once Nana doesn't have to nag me at dinner to tell her something about my day. I've got Lucy's news to share.

This is something Nana understands. "I'm so sorry, honeybee."

"They're having a goodbye dinner this weekend," I say. "Is it okay if I go?"

"Of course." Nana looks thoughtful. She seems kind of far away. Maybe she's thinking about how long it's going to be before she can go anywhere without having to make sure that the place has sloped curbs and handicap-accessible bathrooms.

"Is your leg hurting you?" I ask.

Nana comes back to herself and nods. "I hurt in a lot of different places. My back is stiff, my butt is stiff. Wheelchairs aren't very comfortable. Or maybe it's just this one. And, yes, my leg hurts too. I hate to take those painkillers the doctor prescribed. Some of them are very addictive. You know that, right?"

I just nod. Of course I know that. Nana never lets an opportunity go by to remind me how addictive drugs can be. How much trouble they can get someone into. We had a big assembly at school last fall about drugs and they didn't say a single thing I didn't already know. I could have gotten up and given the big speech myself.

I'm just thankful Nana is skipping *that* talk.

"Did you do anything special today, Nana?"

"I watched *Ironside*." That show was never Nana's favorite, but since her injury she's gotten more interested in it.

"That show is not realistic," I remind her.

Nana drops her fork into her empty frozen dinner box and leans back, wiggling her shoulders and trying to find a more comfortable position. "Why didn't you tell me about what happened with the toilet yesterday afternoon?"

Ugh.

"How did you find out about that?" I ask.

"That was Ruben's mom on the phone just now. She called to apologize about the flood, and to say that if we want to call a plumber, she's sure we can take the cost off next month's rent.

She was pretty surprised I didn't know anything about it. And I was too. Why didn't you tell me?"

Does Ruben have to tell his parents *everything*?

I try a shrug. "Ruben and I took care of it."

Nana keeps looking at me.

"Nana, I don't know why I didn't tell you. I guess I didn't want to bug you with it."

Finally Nana nods. She starts reaching for our plates. She says that at least she can clear the table and load the dishwasher. But the truth is, even that isn't easy. It takes her about three times as long as it would take me, and her stuck-out leg gets in the way the whole time. She bangs it against one of the chairs and uses a word that would get me grounded for two days. "How long am I going to be in this thing?"

"Two months, right?"

We look at each other. You can't ever be sure you're having the same thought as another person, but I'm pretty sure Nana and I are thinking the same thing right now: we've been doing this for less than a week, and we're already pretty tired of it.

After the dishwasher is loaded, Nana rolls down the hall toward the bathroom. We've found out that Nana's shower works better at night now. That way I'm around to help her out if she needs it. I go downstairs, fold more towels, and then put the last batch of towels into the dryer.

I'm almost caught up.

I feel a surge of hope. Nana and I can do this!

I carry the clean towels up the stairs and into the hall just in time to see a whoosh of water coming out from under the bathroom door.

Nana shouts out a word that would get me grounded for a month.

CHAPTER 7

THE NEXT AFTERNOON, I come home with a bagful of groceries and what feels like enough homework for six people. At least the math is done. I dropped in at Homework Club to make sure.

Nana blinks and struggles up into a sitting position on the sofa. She must have taken some of her painkillers today. She reaches over for her wheelchair, and I go and hold it for her while she gets into it. "I'm starved. What are we having for dinner?"

Lately she asks this question every night. I don't look forward to it. "It's either frozen dinners or breakfast."

"We had frozen dinners yesterday, and you know I don't like breakfast for dinner."

"Look," I hear myself say as I pull groceries out of the bag, "I *asked* whether I could go to that cooking camp last summer with Ruben and you said it was too expensive and there wasn't a bus and you'd have to drive me there. So don't blame me!"

"It *was* really expensive," my nana says, but in a quieter voice than I expected. "Fine. I guess we can have breakfast."

"There are frozen waffles," I say, trying to sound like they're a special treat. I swear, I sound like those moms I've seen in the park trying to get their toddlers to leave the swings and come home for lunch.

There are dirty dishes on the counter, and I pop open the dishwasher to get them loaded in. The dishes from last night are still in there. "Nana, you were supposed to empty the dishwasher today."

Nana sighs. "Come on, honeybee, give me a break. It's so hard for me to unload it with my leg like this. It takes me forever, and you can do it in about five minutes."

"It's your responsibility—" I start. And then I stop.

We look at each other.

I can't help it, I laugh. We both do.

She wheels over to the dishwasher, opens it, and gets herself in position to unload the dishes. First she puts the dishes up on the counter and when there's no more room for them, she puts those dishes away before getting back to unloading the next round from the dishwasher. It's tedious, but it works. While she's doing that, I start scrambling eggs and toasting waffles. I slice up some bananas too.

"How was school?" Nana asks when we sit down to eat.

"Fine. How was your day?"

Nana sighs. "Boring."

I spear a piece of waffle and drag it through the puddle of syrup on my plate. I'm starting to understand why Nana is not

61

sympathetic when I say I'm bored. It feels like a long time since I had nothing to do.

"Franny, what do you think about Uncle Gabe coming to stay for a while?"

I freeze with my fork in midair, like someone in a cartoon. "Who?"

"Your uncle Gabe."

Nana almost never talks about my mom's younger brother. When she does, the comments aren't usually nice ones. Even when she's talking about something good that's happened to him, she has a way of putting it down. Gabe has some "big new job," she'll say. Gabe is driving some "hotshot new car." Well, she'll say, Gabe and "that girlfriend of his" broke up.

I wouldn't know Uncle Gabe if I walked by him on the street. I'm not sure I've even seen a picture of him. We're not a big family for photos. Nana still has an old camera that needs film. It's kind of a pain in the butt to use, and she doesn't get it out very often.

"Mr. Burns called me today, and we had a discussion about how things are going. A few of your teachers have reached out to him."

I can't believe Mr. Burns and my teachers are snitching me out!

I'm doing the best I can!

"Now, I'm not mad. Neither is he. He just said you seem

to be having a little more trouble at school staying on top of things. Something about forgetting some homework? And not doing very well on your makeup math quiz? I hate to see that happen, after all the work we put in to get you caught up in math."

Nana's right about that. I was really proud of myself when I got into regular math instead of remedial. Nana was so happy, we went out to dinner in the middle of the week and she bought me a big box of oil pastels.

Nana says, "I talked to Gracie about it. She said it sounded like you were keeping a lot of balls in the air for a twelve-year-old. Mr. Burns said the same thing. You know, they're both right."

I look around the house. I guess you can't exactly call our kitchen clean and tidy. There's rice all over the floor, and the last time we had rice was when we ordered Chinese. And this table is greasy, like maybe some butter got on it.

"Maybe there are people who help out with things like this for money?"

"There are, but that can add up fast and get expensive. I'm paying rent on two places right now. Your uncle's a programmer. I'm pretty sure working remotely won't be a problem for him for a month or two. It's just until I get out of this wheelchair and into that hinged-brace thingy. Everyone in the support group says it all gets easier then."

"Support group?" I say.

"Oh, just this online knee injury support group Gracie found on Facebook. I thought it was going to be a total waste of time, but the people on there are actually pretty helpful. I know we can make it once I'm out of this wheelchair, but we need a little help in the meantime."

"Where's he going to stay?" I ask. "There are only two bedrooms."

"There's that bedroom in the basement off the garage. He can have that."

"Nana, it's really dark and depressing down there!"

"Honeybee, let me tell you a story. When you were a baby, you and your mom lived in a basement apartment in Somerville, Massachusetts, that was so horrible your poppy called it 'the groundhog den.' It had two tiny windows and a concrete floor, and the ceiling was so low he could barely stand upright in it! And your uncle said he thought it sounded 'fine.' Fine, for your mom and you, a two-month-old baby." Nana's eyes snap with frosty sparks. "He can see how *he* likes living in a basement."

Somerville?

I thought Mom and I lived in Boston.

Nana almost never tells stories from when I was little. I'm torn between asking more about Somerville and protesting about Uncle Gabe. "But, Nana—"

64

"I'm talking to your uncle tonight," Nana says.

"That's not fair!" From everything I've heard about him, unselfish caregiving doesn't sound like his thing. "You told me we were talking about this. Not that you already made up your mind. Doesn't it matter what I think? I don't even know Uncle Gabe."

"Well," my nana says, "I guess you're going to get your chance."

The moment dinner is over, Nana has me find her phone, which she leaves in all kinds of strange places, and rolls down the hallway to her bedroom. I can hear her talking while I load the dishwasher and sweep away the rice and get all the grease off our table. By the time I'm squeezing out the dishcloth, Nana is back in the living room. "Franny, can you help me get on the sofa?"

Once she's safely installed there, I hand her the TV remote. It's just another Thursday night in our house. Any moment, Nana will be clicking through the local PBS stations. "What did Uncle Gabe say?"

"He's coming Monday."

"Monday? Are you serious?"

You need to understand, Nana never moves this fast. She likes to take things in her own good time. Even a change like trying a new diner for lunch or buying a new color of scrubs for work—Nana will think it over.

"We need the help now. Not a week from now. No reason to put it off." Nana almost sounds as if she wishes my uncle had come up with some reason.

"And he'll be here for two months?"

"That's the plan." Nana turns on the TV.

I raise my voice to be heard over *PBS NewsHour*. "What do you mean, Nana?"

"Let's say I have my doubts about the visit lasting that long. Two months is a lot of togetherness for your uncle and me."

And Nana scolds *me* about having a bad attitude.

～๑

THE NEXT DAY AT lunch, as usual, Ruben announces the weekend Game Day plan. "My house, Sunday afternoon, two o'clock. Who's in? If we have enough people, we could have two Catan games going!"

That happened, like, one time, but ever since, it's been Ruben's standard of a successful gaming event.

Eliot Dreyer nods, and Arun Banerjee nods too. They show up pretty much every Sunday. But a lot of the other regulars have plans already, for whatever reason. Forget having eight people—this is going to be one of those weekends when Ruben has trouble scraping up four.

I bite into my pizza and try to act like I'm busy thinking about something important.

Ruben says, "Franny?"

"Rubes, I've got so much to do this weekend."

"You're always there on Sunday."

"I know, but my uncle is coming on Monday to help out for a while." I'm still wrapping my mind around that, but he'll be here whether I'm used to the idea or not. "He's supposed to stay in the basement, and I need to get his room ready. Nana can't do it."

(She also has no interest in doing it.)

(Her only remark on the topic has been, "If your uncle doesn't like it, he can find a hotel.")

Ruben grins and peels the foil off the top of his pudding cup. "Oh. That's good! My mom and dad were wondering when someone from your family was going to show up."

I crumple my napkin into a ball. Sometimes it just feels like Ruben and I live in two different worlds. It's like the setup of one of those fantasy novels he loves. They overlap, and you can travel from one to the other. But they're two different places, and sometimes I wonder if the gateway between them will close someday and never open again.

"But that still leaves us short one person," Ruben says.

"I can ask Tate Grady if he wants to come," Eliot says. "We're in the same math class, and he's a total gamer. What do you think, Arun?"

Arun pushes his glasses up and hesitates before he says, "I mean, he'll spend the whole time bragging about his Pokémon cards and telling the rest of us what we're doing wrong, but I guess it's okay."

"Awesome!" Ruben says. He points a fake-threatening finger at me and says, "You're off the hook."

SUNDAY NIGHT DINNER IS canned tomato soup, cheese toast, and salad that I pull out of a plastic box. I have a glass of milk and Nana has tap water.

The food seems even grimmer than usual because, before Nana hurt her knee, Sunday was the day when she'd make a really nice dinner. She'd break out one of the containers of Sunday sauce she keeps in the freezer and cook up a pasta feast.

I would have tried to make something better, but I spent all day down in the basement getting everything ready for Uncle Gabe. My hair is full of cobwebs, and when I washed my hands, the water in the sink turned gray. There was a whole lot of dust down there.

Nana pushes away her soup after just a few spoonfuls.

"Is the soup okay?" I ask.

"I'm just sick of food out of cans and boxes."

I feel embarrassed I'm not a better cook. But I also feel kind of annoyed. As I've already pointed out to Nana, it's not my fault I can't cook. "Well, I'm sorry," I say.

Nana doesn't say anything nice like "It's certainly not your fault" or "This isn't so bad." She nibbles a little of the cheese toast, then puts it down and pushes away her plate.

"Maybe Uncle Gabe will cook all kinds of good stuff," I say.

Nana snorts, the way she always does when the subject of my uncle comes up. "He could burn water back when I saw him in action. Then again, I haven't seen him in years." And then she adds, like all this wasn't bad enough, "I hope I recognize him."

"Nana . . . "

"*What*," my nana says.

Man, is she in a terrible mood.

"Um. I think we should be nice when Uncle Gabe gets here. I mean, he is helping us out."

Nana looks grumpy, but at least she doesn't start arguing with me.

I think of everything Dr. Yao does when their family has people coming to stay in their guest room, which happens a lot. Old friends. Colleagues in town. Relatives from the West Coast or the Philippines.

She cleans the bathroom, she puts out fresh sheets and towels. I already did that.

She buys flowers. We don't usually have flowers, but I could go by the market and get some.

And, a lot of times, she has a party.

The Yaos had a big one when Ruben's grandparents came to visit last year. It went on all day, music and food and people chatting up a storm. It was super fun. When Nana came to pick me up, she stayed for a while and had a drink and a plateful of barbecue. She was laughing and talking. I wish I saw Nana laugh more.

"I think maybe we should have a party. To welcome him and let him know we're grateful."

Nana drops her spoon and it clatters onto the table. "A *party*?"

I don't blame her for being surprised. I've surprised myself. We don't have parties. I'm not sure why. Nana's idea of a big celebration is having someone over for dinner. And by "someone," I mean one person. Like Aunt Gravy.

But other people have parties. Not just the Yaos. Lucy's family has parties too. Ned's bar mitzvah was the fanciest party I've ever been to. It was in a private room at a hotel in New York City. They had a sit-down dinner and a DJ, and we got gifts just for being there. I guess becoming a bar mitzvah is hard work, and a lot of people like to really throw down and celebrate. That's what Lucy says, anyway. She started Hebrew school this year.

"A party," I repeat to Nana now. "You know, you have people over and have food and drinks and music and they all have fun."

"I'm familiar with the concept," Nana says dryly. "But how are we going to make this happen? Parties are a lot of *work*. You have to clean, you have to get things ready—"

"I can take care of all that," I tell her.

"We'd need food and drink, and I'm not sure who we would even invite. Who would we ask?"

"The Yaos," I say right away. "They have me over all the time, and they did more for us than anyone when you hurt your leg."

"That's true." Nana pushes her hands into her hair, the way she does when she's thinking. "Get me a piece of paper and a pen. Let's see. Adela, Tom—"

(Tom is Mr. Yao, Ruben's dad.)

"Reyna and Ruben—" Nana goes on.

I wish Lucy were still here. She likes parties and she can talk to anyone. "I could ask Eliot and Arun."

Nana knows their names from my descriptions of Game Day afternoons. She writes them down too. "Dr. Morgenstern and Dr. Lee. They won't come, but it's nice to ask them. Gracie, of course. And the rest of the girls from the practice . . . "

"Nana, *not* Aunt Gravy," I protest, before I can think.

Nana pauses her pencil to stare at me and doesn't stop staring until I meet her gaze.

"No Grace, no party," she says.

Okay, okay. I don't say anything more about Aunt Gracie. I change the subject. "We're going to need music. The Yaos always play music at their parties."

"That's what the radio is for," Nana says, spearing up another piece of waffle. "I'll start calling people after dinner. It's short notice, but I'm sure some of them will be able to come."

"Maybe I should go by the apartment and get your CDs," I offer. "You'd probably like having them here anyway."

Yup, Nana is so old-school, she still plays her music on CDs. I do too, because as previously mentioned, I have no phone. Luckily Mr. Tan was the same as Nana, and the living room stereo has a CD player.

"It would be nice to be able to play music in the afternoon." Nana's grin appears. She's about to start teasing. "Are my CDs the only things you want to get from the apartment?"

There's no fooling Nana. "I was going to bring over some more of my art stuff."

When we packed up to move into this house, Nana convinced me to leave most of my art supplies behind. I brought some paper and paints and my best colored pencils. But I left the boxes where I stash my pieces of bark and cool-shaped branches and single socks and all the things that fall off cars and get left on the side of the road. You know, those things. My found objects.

(There's also the kite, which Nana doesn't know about yet because I stashed it in my closet before she got home.)

"Fine, you can get the CDs and some of your bits and pieces. But you're going to need to take the shopping cart. That's way too much for you to carry home."

This is Nana's revenge. I hate our wheelie cart. It's one of those tall wire boxes on wheels that you see people in the city use sometimes. When I use it, it makes me look like a total dweeb, or like someone who's one hundred years old.

IT'S NOT UNTIL A few hours later when I flip open my journal and write down *Things Currently Worrying Franny Petroski* that I realize what I've done.

We're having a party.

Us.

I've never had a party. And I've never helped anyone else throw a party either. A few people over for my birthday doesn't really count, and we stopped doing that a few years ago anyway.

I end up writing:

PARTY NEXT WEEKEND?!!!!!!!!!!!!!

I write it in all capitals and so big, it takes up the whole line. Then I add:

Please don't let the toilet clog.

CHAPTER 8

THE NEXT DAY, I wake up worrying. I carry on worrying all the way into school and through my morning classes.

If I could get a few minutes to write down some Things Currently Worrying Franny Petroski, it would help empty out my brain, but this is one of those mornings when all the teachers are determined not to give us a minute of free time.

"This will be on the quiz this Friday—"

"Take out your books and turn to page 129—"

"Get into your small groups—"

Mr. Burns likes to say, "There are other ways of taking care of things besides worrying about them." Sometimes that advice helps my head slow down. It's true that making lists and prioritizing things and trying to get a few small things done every day is better than just freezing up and doing nothing. But not today. My mind is still spinning when I go to lunch at eleven thirty.

That's just when Uncle Gabe's airplane is supposed to touch down.

I hurry to the cafeteria because Ruben is always the first one at our table and I want to catch him alone. He's already slurping up pancit noodles and looking at something on his phone—probably a chess puzzle.

When I sit down next to him, he says, "Sorry. It's got pork today."

A lot of times Ruben brings veggie pancit so I can have some. And also because his mom, like pretty much every other mom in the world, thinks he should eat more vegetables.

"It's okay." I look down at my soggy grilled cheese, which lets me know it's Monday, just in case I'd forgotten. "But I do have a question."

He looks at me. Ruben likes questions. He likes answering them, he likes asking them, he likes thinking about them. He just likes them in general.

"What kind of food does your mom have at her parties?"

"Oh, I heard about that party your nana is having next weekend. Mom said she didn't know you guys had parties."

"Are you coming?" I ask.

"Sure," Ruben says, like I should have known this already. "Let me think. Mom makes chicken adobo a lot for parties. Lechón, that's roast pork. Lumpia—"

Lumpia are like egg rolls and they're excellent, but I know from being around Ruben's parents that you have to do a lot of chopping with sharp knives and they also involve a huge pot of hot fat. I'm not ready for that.

"Isn't your nana going to do the food?" Ruben asks me.

"She's getting some stuff, but . . . "

Nana and I don't agree about the food.

Nana's idea of party food is a few party platters from the supermarket and some bottles of drinks. Aunt Gracie is picking it all up for us. When I think of the parties I've been to, or even seen while I walked by them on the street or spied on them from my bedroom window, it seems like they have way more food and way more exciting food and people seem hyped about eating it.

Nana shrugged when I told her this and told me to knock myself out if I wanted anything fancier.

She doesn't usually talk to me like that. I think she's cranky because Uncle Gabe is coming. What I don't know is why.

"I just want to do something a little extra," I say to Ruben.

"I can ask Mom to bring some lumpia if you want. She's probably already planning to do that anyway. Mom always brings something."

Eliot and Arun smack their trays down and sit.

"What are you guys talking about?" Eliot unwraps his silverware.

"Food for Franny's party on Saturday," Ruben says.

"I can ask my mom if I can bring something," Eliot says. "Mom says the best parties are always potluck anyway. She usually brings shepherd's pie."

"I can ask my parents if I can bring samosas," Arun says.

"Although, to be honest, Mom and Dad might just buy them at Patel's. Mom always says people have lives."

"Franny doesn't eat meat," Ruben reminds them, being a little bossy the way he can be sometimes, because I usually don't bother telling people. There's always something I can eat.

"*What?!*" someone says.

This kid I don't know smacks his tray onto the table next to Ruben's and sits down like he does this every day instead of it being the first time.

He says, "Who doesn't eat *meat*? That's like the cornerstone of my diet!"

"Tate, hey," Ruben says, and fist-bumps him. The kid fist-bumps him right back and unwraps his fork and knife.

So this must be Tate Grady. I guess he and Ruben hit it off at Game Day yesterday. Tate has wire-rim glasses and messy shoulder-length dark hair. His T-shirt is advertising Middle Earth's Annual Mordor Fun Run. No wonder Ruben likes him.

Arun says, "Dude, it's not that weird to be a vegetarian."

Eliot says, "Meatless is no problem. My mom makes a great veggie shepherd's pie. She's always after me to eat more vegetables."

See what I mean about mothers?

Most people's moms, anyway.

"I'm still wondering what I should make," I say.

"What's your specialty?" Arun asks.

That's my problem. I don't have a special dish unless you count cheese toast or frozen waffles.

"Here's an idea," Eliot says, "make a nice dessert. My mom says whenever she doesn't know what to bring, she does a nice dessert. The kind of dessert that makes everyone's mouth start watering the moment they see it."

I like that idea.

AFTER SCHOOL ENDS, I wait a few minutes for everyone to clear out before going to the art room to get our wheelie cart. (I'd left it in there this morning. It wasn't in the way there, and Miss Midori said she didn't mind.)

I drag it downtown. It rattles the entire way, I swear, and the old bungee cords wrapped around its handle bounce along like they're keeping time. School buses keep passing me. I'm pretty sure everyone in our middle school has had a chance to see me with the cart by the time I finally get to our apartment.

The guys at Java Dream wave at me as I check our mailbox. There are a few flyers that look like junk mail and the weekly coupons from the market. There's one postcard, kind of vintage-looking. It's a picture of a big building, like a cathedral, in a snowstorm, and the caption says: SNOWY SALT LAKE CITY. It's for Nana, of course. I never get mail. The message on the other side says, *Just got back and already FREEZING! Heading for Arizona stat!*

Whoever wrote this card made the word "FREEZING" super large and drew icicles hanging from it.

Nana gets postcards like these once in a while. She says that some of her old friends travel a lot now that they're retired. It's weird they never sign the cards, but people can be weird in general.

Anyway. I put the mail in my backpack, unlock our front door, and go upstairs. It's funny how I see everything now from the perspective of Nana's wheelchair and stuck-out leg. The downstairs landing is a tight little space even for someone who's not in a wheelchair, and our stairs are pretty narrow too. I don't think Nana could do them even on crutches. I guess we're going to be in Mr. Tan's house for a while longer.

I take a quick look around the apartment. The oven is off, the fridge is cold inside, and the toilet is flushing. I don't know why I feel like I have to check the toilet. Maybe the toilet in our rental house has me worrying about every single one I come across now.

I put the two shoeboxes of Nana's CDs in the cart and then go down to my room. I open my closet and look over that dusty kite from the bushes outside school. I hauled it home just a little over a week ago. It seems like longer, with everything that's happened since then.

Is it junk yet?

That's what Nana says sometimes, when I'm hanging on to

something she thinks is trash and she wants to know whether it can be thrown out.

Nope, not yet.

If I had it at Mr. Tan's house, where I would see it now and then, maybe I could figure out what to use it for. I prop it up next to the wheelie cart and go back to open Nana's door and check her room. Her bed is made, her room is tidy, the way Nana likes it. But it smells a little dusty. I can tell no one's been in here for a while.

I can head home now. Everything checks out.

But I don't leave.

Instead I step inside Nana's room.

I'm not exactly breaking a rule. When I was little and had lots of nightmares, I was in here all the time. But when I was older and started sleeping well, Nana's bedroom turned into her personal space. And I don't mind. Because my room is my personal space too. Nana always knocks on my bedroom door before she comes in, and she doesn't snoop. Lucy could never leave *her* journal out on top of her bureau. If her mum didn't peek in it to make sure Lucy was doing okay, one of her brothers would be checking out her business.

Here's an embarrassing thing about me. When I first started living with Nana, I used to hide food in my closet. I had to have a private stash in case I got hungry. I knew it was silly, and we always had food, but I needed it. Well, Nana never touched that stash or talked about it, and I know she knew it was there, because a few times we got ants and had to clean it all out. I don't have to do that anymore, but I always remember Nana was cool about it.

So I feel bad snooping around Nana's room. But here I am doing it. I don't know why. Maybe it's just that I can get away with it. For once, there's no chance of Nana coming home early and surprising me.

Or maybe it has to do with Nana never wanting to talk about Mom, or how things were when I lived with Mom. Until a few days ago, I didn't know I had ever lived in a place called Somerville, let alone in a basement apartment so sad and dark that someone would call it a groundhog den. Sometimes I want to know more about me and Mom, even if I don't admit it. Even if I act like I don't care.

The pictures on Nana's bureau haven't changed. Here's a picture of Nana and Poppy on their wedding day. Nana looks pretty in a lacy dress and matching veil and Poppy is smiling so wide I can't look at him without grinning myself. There are a few school portraits of me, which I don't bother looking at because I know what I look like already, and that sunflower painting I made Nana.

That's it.

No pictures of my mom. None of my mom and me. None of Uncle Gabe, either.

I open Nana's closet. On the shelf above the closet rod there are some brown storage boxes. But now that I'm taller, I can see those aren't the only things up there. There's stuff behind those boxes.

I grab the step stool and climb up. I shove the brown boxes aside.

There's a portable record player, like a little suitcase with a handle. This one is turquoise-colored, and beside it there's a matching turquoise-colored box that's pretty heavy. When I pull that box out and climb down with it to have a closer look, it's full of record albums.

I pull one out.

I remember this album cover.

It's abstract. There are different shades of orange and yellow and black rectangles. It's really joyful. *Getz/Gilberto*, the album says at the top. I'm suddenly humming a song. This old jazz standard called "The Girl from Ipanema."

When I flip over the album, I see "The Girl from Ipanema" is the first side.

I'm not kidding.

These are Mom's albums.

Of course she had lots of jazz albums. Nana has told me Mom wanted to be a jazz vocalist, although she never says anything more after that. It always turns into one of those "Let's talk about that some other time" things.

That matching portable record player, that's Mom's record player.

I have a faint memory of lying on the floor in front of it while music played. I remember the smell of dust and Mom lying next to me. I think I remember her singing along softly.

Why didn't I know they were here?

I drag out the portable record player and let it join the box of albums on the floor.

These were Mom's. And as far as I'm concerned, that means they're mine now. Nana had no right to never tell me they were here!

Sneezing, I climb back up and pull out something else from behind the boxes.

It's a purple duffel bag.

It's a purple duffel bag that smells like my mom.

How do I know that?

I just do.

I get dizzy and have to hold on to the side of the closet while I climb down. I put the duffel on the bed and unzip it. Mom's clothes are inside.

I know they are Mom's because they smell like her too. And when I pull the clothes out, some of them give me more sparks of memories. The scratchy sequins on this pink tunic. The fringe on that long turquoise scarf. I remember the shape of that coffee stain on these jeans, and I think I even remember that stain happening, Mom jumping up to yell about something, coffee knocked over and splashing onto her lap.

I remember I felt scared, and like I had to be very quiet. Mom wasn't yelling at me. She never yelled at me. But that didn't mean she couldn't be scary sometimes.

All of a sudden I wonder how late it is.

I push the clothes back into Mom's duffel. I'm taking that, too.

Between the duffel, the record player and albums, and Nana's CDs, the cart is just about full. I'll have to come back another time for my art supplies. I straighten up Nana's closet and put the step stool back by her winter boots, and then I smooth out some wrinkles on the bed. The room looks the way it should look, but that doesn't mean Nana won't know I've been in here hunting around. She has a sixth sense for things like that.

I'll deal with that later.

There's just enough room to stick the kite on top of everything else. And then it's time to drag the whole thing home and hope no one else from school sees me.

CHAPTER 9

AT HOME, I GO straight through the garage into the basement, where I know Nana won't be, and I unload the cart. I dust off a shelf by the washing machine and put the duffel there, along with the albums and record player. The kite gets propped up against the wall.

I don't hear anything from upstairs. No footsteps or people chatting or the TV—nothing. I wonder whether my uncle is even here. Don't flights get delayed sometimes?

I take the shoeboxes of CDs and the handful of mail and I go upstairs.

This silence wouldn't be weird if my nana were alone. It's weird because my nana *isn't* alone.

Nana is flipping through an *Architectural Digest* I know she's read before. (Dr. Morgenstern brought by a massive stack of old magazines from the dental office.)

My uncle is across from her in the old prickly armchair that smells like every cat that ever slept on it.

He's big. He's tall and he's wide across. Not fat—just solid. He has Mom's caramel-colored hair, but less of it, and blue eyes like hers. His glasses are round and rad. His face reminds me of my mom's—a long straight nose, full lips, and the same ears. If you'd asked me, I would have said I don't remember Mom's face. I was only four when I came to live with Nana. But somehow I know Uncle Gabe looks like Mom. I'm sure of it. It's a very strange feeling, and it's hard to stop looking at him.

It's like smelling Mom's clothes all over again.

I put the CDs and mail on the kitchen counter.

Nana lets her magazine flop down. "Hey, honeybee."

I wish Nana wouldn't call me "honeybee" in front of strangers. We've talked about this!

Then again, is Uncle Gabe a stranger? He is my uncle, even if I don't know him at all. Anyway, he ignores "honeybee," thank God. He doesn't smile when Nana says it. Not one twitch at the corners of his mouth.

"Say hi to your uncle Gabriel. Gabe, this is Franny."

He says, "Hi, Franny. I met you once, but it was years ago. You're about four times as tall as you were then."

"Not too surprising, given that she was one year old the last time you saw her," Nana says.

I didn't know Uncle Gabe and I had met. Nana sure never mentioned it.

Uncle Gabe asks, "How old are you now?"

"Twelve." Just to avoid the inevitable next question, I add, "I'm in sixth grade."

"Ah," my uncle says. "Middle school."

Just the way he says "middle school" tells me that he remembers a lot about it and he sympathizes with its crappier aspects.

I try to think of what to say next. "Um, how was your flight?"

"It was fine, thanks."

That's it. I can't think of any more small talk.

Nana says, "I see you got my CDs. Did everything look okay in the apartment?"

I nod yes.

"Good. You left the shopping cart in the basement?"

"It's by the washing machine."

The silence comes back.

I go into the kitchen and make myself a sandwich. I can practically hear my knife spreading the peanut butter. I wonder why Nana doesn't turn on the radio. It's like she's punishing all of us with this silence. "Does anyone else want something?"

"I'm okay," my grandmother and uncle say at the same time. They look at each other. My uncle smiles. My nana does not smile. She purses her lips and goes back to her magazine.

"What are we having for dinner?" I ask. Just to say something.

"I was thinking takeout," Uncle Gabe says.

"Oooh, that sounds good," I say at the same moment Nana says, "Takeout? You're not cooking?"

Uncle Gabe closes his eyes. "No, Ma, I wasn't planning on cooking tonight. I haven't thought about what to make and I haven't gotten any groceries."

"The grocery store is just two blocks away," Nana says. "Toward uptown. Franny's been *walking* there and back."

"I just got off a plane. Let's have takeout. I'll go to the store tomorrow. Okay?"

"Fine."

Uncle Gabe glances around. "This looks like a nice place."

Nana looks as if that's the most idiotic lie she ever heard—and this is Nana, who has to ask people whether they floss regularly. She says coldly, "Well, to be honest, it's kind of a dump, but we're managing."

A dump? I look around. Maybe it's not fancy, but I think it's okay, now that we've worked out the toilet situation. The rooms are bigger than the apartment's and there are more windows and outside there are trees and grass instead of parking lots and brick walls.

"How's the old house, Mom? You ever go by? Is it still there?"

Old house? What old house? Then I figure Uncle Gabe must be talking about the house where he and Mom grew up. It's in Livingston, a few towns east of here.

"Why would I?" Nana flips a page. "We haven't lived there for years, and it's a bit of a drive."

"It's not that far. Maybe Franny would like to see it."

I sure would. When Uncle Gabe looks at me, I nod furiously. "Might be cool to see what it looks like now," I offer.

Nana says nothing.

I eat my sandwich over the sink. I can hear myself chewing. I wonder if my nana and uncle can too.

My uncle gets up and stretches. "You know, I think I'll go downstairs and finish unpacking."

"Fine."

"I guess we can order dinner around six, unless you want it earlier."

Nana shrugs. Uncle Gabe looks at me with something on his face that's almost like pleading. I rush to say, "Sounds great to me!"

I sound like the girls from student government, who flash big smiles and put exclamation points at the end of everything they say. Kind of chirpy.

Uncle Gabe walks down the hall to the basement door.

My nana turns another page with a snap.

"I guess I'll go and finish my French," I say.

I pick up my backpack and head down the hall, but when I pass the basement door, I stop. I remember something. When the Yaos have overnight guests, Dr. Yao always *shows* them the guest room. She points out the closet and bathroom and makes sure they have everything they need. I've seen her do it. She's done it with me.

I look back at Nana. She's staring out the picture window. I'm pretty sure that, even if her leg were working right, she wouldn't go downstairs with Uncle Gabe to make sure he was comfortable.

This is going to be a long two months if every day is like this.

I foresee a lot of time at Ruben's if he isn't too busy.

If only Lucy were still here! I know she'd get it.

I go downstairs.

Uncle Gabe's door is open. He's lying on the bed, propped up on the pillows, looking at his phone. "Oh! Franny, hi."

"I just wanted to make sure you had everything you need."

"Thanks, it's great. I haven't seen one of these in a long time." He runs his hand over the candlewick bedspread.

"I think there's an extra one upstairs if you want a different one—"

"No, no. It's cool. Kind of nostalgic. I think my grandmother or my great-aunt had one of these."

"I think so," I say, remembering Mom rubbing my hand over the bedspread. I look around. On top of the dresser, there's a laptop covered with stickers and a bundle of cords and chargers. The closet door is slightly open and I can see shirts hung up inside. He sure looks unpacked to me.

Uncle Gabe says, "I just needed a break. Your grandmother and I are not off to the best start."

That surprises me. The Uncle Gabe my nana has painted over the years would never say something like that.

"She always was a fan of the silent treatment when we had disappointed her. I guess some things don't change."

I'm not sure what to say.

"There are fresh towels in the bathroom," I manage.

"Oh! I noticed that. Thanks." He takes off his glasses and rubs his eyes.

"I'd like to see the house you grew up in," I confess. "That Mom grew up in."

"Ma never drove you over there? Seriously? It's not that far. A half hour on I-80 and you're there." Uncle Gabe rubs his chin, like he's thinking. "Hey, I've got an idea. I was going to go out tomorrow and do some shopping for electronics. I need better Wi-Fi if I'm going to get any work done, for one thing. I was going to go tomorrow morning, but I could put it off till the afternoon. We could take a drive past the house after I'm done. What time is school over tomorrow?"

"Three!" I practically shout it.

"Okay, wait for me outside by the front door. Does that work?"

"Yes!" I swear, I am turning into one of those chirpy girls. "Thanks!"

"No problem—honeybee." Uncle Gabe grins.

CHAPTER 10

AFTER SCHOOL THE NEXT day I'm one of the first kids out the door, but Uncle Gabe is already there, standing with his back to the cold breeze, a phone in his hand. He has AirPods in and a funny look on his face, like he's thinking hard.

"Hi, Uncle Gabe!"

Uncle Gabe frowns and says, "Just a moment, people." He pulls an AirPod out of one ear and says, "I'm in a meeting right now. You'll need to pipe down until we get to the store. Capeesh?"

"Capeesh" is a Jersey thing—everyone around here knows that "Capeesh?" means "You get it?" or "You understand?" in Italian.

"Sorry," I whisper.

We walk to the car and ride to the mall in a weird silence broken only by Uncle Gabe saying, "I'm not sure the network is configured for that kind of usage" and "That deadline works for now, but we need to revisit after we have more information."

Uncle Gabe talks about configuring networks and revisiting deadlines.

Nana talks about gum recessions and root canals.

Sometimes I worry being an adult isn't going to be a whole bunch of fun.

But when we park the car, Uncle Gabe says, "That's fine, let's touch base later," and reaches up to take the AirPods out of his ears. He stows them in their capsule and puts the capsule in the glove compartment. Then he turns to smile at me. It's like he's back.

I almost never go inside these big electronic stores, but Uncle Gabe is totally at home. First we stop in the aisle with Wi-Fi equipment. Uncle Gabe knows exactly what he wants. He tucks the box under his arm and then he surprises me by saying, "Let's go look at phones while we're here."

I'd really like to have a phone. Nana says there's absolutely no reason for me to have one until I'm in high school, and then she'll probably just give me her old one.

That'll be mega exciting.

I'm not sure you can even *text* on Nana's phone.

Uncle Gabe explains, "I need a new one. My phone is way out-of-date. It's been freezing up and having problems installing new apps and junk like that."

Looking at the new phones is like shopping in the best candy store ever. I could wander around checking them out forever, so it's too bad Uncle Gabe knows exactly what he wants here, too. He takes the box from the salesclerk. Then he slows down and takes another look at all the phones spread out under the display glass.

"Does your nana still use that old flip phone from 1990 or something?" he asks me.

"I don't know how old it is, but it's old," I tell him. "She's had the same one for as long as I can remember."

Uncle Gabe drums his fingers on the counter. The salesclerk waits with a tolerant smile. He's a tall lean guy with a knot of locs on top of his head and his fingernails are painted black. He's basically the person I want to be when I grow up, a cool art kid. I can't wait until I can do fingernail polish. Nana says when I turn thirteen, I can start playing around more with nail polish and makeup and my hair. I don't care about makeup. Lucy and I mess around with her mom's stash sometimes. I don't like the way it feels on my face, and I hate the way hair spray smells. But nail polish is cool. I can't wait to have my favorite colors on my fingernails whenever I want. I'm going to do orange first. And when I'm eighteen, I'm piercing my nose, and I don't care how much Nana freaks out about it.

"You know what, give me another one of these phones," my uncle finally says.

"My man!" The clerk gives me a faint wink. He dives under the counter for another box.

I just about faint. That's what Nana would call, in her disapproving way, "a *lot* of money."

I'm also not sure how she is going to feel about a new phone. Nana can be funny about things like that. She says that just because something is new doesn't make it better, and that the world is going so fast nowadays it makes her dizzy and she wishes it would slow down.

"Could you do me a favor?" my uncle asks the clerk. "Could you take these boxes up front and ask them to hold them at the counter? I have one more stop to make."

"Sure, no problem," the clerk says.

I'm feeling uneasy now. What else could Uncle Gabe want to buy? He's going to be spending a buttload of money already!

"Franny, you coming?"

I fake a smile, but I can't make it look excited—just polite. I follow Uncle Gabe toward the TV section. Toward the big, expensive flat-screen TVs, past the huge sign that says, "50% Off! 90-Day Unconditional Guarantee!"

I'm pretty sure Nana is not going to be happy about this.

"You okay?" Uncle Gabe asks me when we are back in the car.

"I'm good."

I'm still stunned by the fact that my uncle just bought a Wi-Fi hub, two new phones, and a flat-screen TV. He just said "Ouch" and handed over his credit card like it was no big deal.

I'm pretty sure I've never seen someone spend that much money before.

I guess Nana was right when she said my uncle had a big job.

"You sure?" Uncle Gabe directs his car up the entrance ramp to the highway and merges onto it easily, like a diver going into a swimming pool. Nana can't do that. She slows down and grips the wheel and usually someone has to take pity on her and slow down to let her in.

The scenery flies by—scrubby trees, shallow ponds, the big electric poles with their wires hanging down and hawks circling overhead. Uncle Gabe fiddles with his phone, making me nervous, and then music starts pouring through the car. This is jazz, but not anything I've heard before.

"Who is this, Uncle Gabe?"

"Esperanza Spalding. You like? Your mom was always more into the old-school classics. I think she thought it meant she was a serious jazz musician. But there are some great new musicians out there."

"I didn't know you liked jazz, Uncle Gabe."

"Jazz was Pops's music," my uncle says. "Jazz and classical were all he wanted to listen to, so we grew up around it."

"I like it too."

"That shows you're a real Petroski. What do you think your nana is going to think about her new phone?"

I sneak him a look. I hope it's okay to tell him the truth. "I'm wondering what Nana's going to think about all these new gadgets."

"Gadgets" is Nana's word.

Uncle Gabe switches lanes with an amazing smoothness. He's frowning. "I guess your nana is dealing with a lot of new stuff already, and that was never her favorite thing."

I never thought of that. But the moment I hear it from Uncle Gabe, I know it's true. It's like a lightbulb coming on. "Yeah! It's kind of weird. Now me, I like new stuff."

"I noticed that too," my uncle says.

We exit the highway. Livingston is a lot like my town, only with everything squished in more tightly together. The yards are smaller, the houses are closer to each other, and the streets are more crowded with cars. Nana says the closer you get to New York City, the more expensive the land is and the more squashed in everything becomes. I guess that makes sense.

There's also a lot more honking. I've noticed honking tends to increase in both volume and frequency the closer you get to the city.

Uncle Gabe drives through the downtown, past a big old-fashioned stone school a lot like mine, and then into a maze of narrow streets just off Livingston Avenue. Now Uncle Gabe is the one who's more and more quiet. Finally he pulls over in front of a house, turns off the ignition, and just sits there. He doesn't say anything.

I have to ask him, "Is this it?"

"This is it." Uncle Gabe isn't smiling now. He looks thoughtful, and also a little stressed. Kind of like someone watching the end of a good scary movie.

"Can I get out and take a look?"

"Knock yourself out."

The house is big and square, with a porch all the way across its front and gable windows on the third floor. I take a few steps into the driveway so I can get a better view of the backyard. I can see a swing set and a new-looking trampoline with a safety net that isn't sagging yet. A wheelbarrow and a soccer ball. It looks like a really nice house, even if it is painted a boring tan color with white trim.

Uncle Gabe comes up beside me. "Those were your mom's windows. Those two." He points to the windows all the way to the left on the second floor. There's a big tree in front of them that keeps me from being able to see inside.

"Is that tree okay?" There's peeling bark all up its trunk.

"It's an American sycamore, so that peeling bark is normal," Uncle Gabe tells me. "That was your mom's favorite tree."

I wander over to take a closer look. The bark stands away from the trunk in big curls. I sneak a look at my uncle, then pull off a few loose pieces and stick them in my coat pockets.

I hear someone call, "Can I help you? Are you looking for someone?"

I look around. A tall blond man with a big mustache like a Western lawman's is standing on the porch of the house next door. He's holding a spoon, like he just came out from a kitchen where he was stirring something.

Uncle Gabe comes up beside me. "I'm sorry. I used to live here, and my niece asked if she could have a look at the place."

He looks more closely at the man on the porch.

Then he says, "Carlton?"

The man looks hard at me, then back at my uncle. "Gabe? Is that you?"

Then their words get all jumbled up together.

"Carlton Ianuzzi! Dude! How long has it been?"

"Are you living here? Last I heard you were out in the Midwest somewhere!"

"How about you? I heard LA?"

Then the tall blond man surprises me. He says, "And is this—Franny?"

How does he know my name? He says it like we know each other.

And then there's the way he's looking at me. It's a little intense. I step closer to Uncle Gabe.

"Oh, so you knew about Mia's venture into motherhood, huh? Yup, this is my niece, Franny. Franny, this is Carlton. We grew up next door to each other, right here."

I give this Carlton person a little wave and then put my hands behind my back like that will keep them from doing anything else that looks stupid.

"Franny, wow," Carlton says. "It's good to see you."

I glance at Uncle Gabe. Carlton seems okay, but I don't really know him. So why is he looking at me like we're long-lost friends?

"I was good friends with your mom," he says. "Best friends, actually."

Now it's my turn to stare. I've never known a friend of my mom's from when she was little.

"She looks like Mia, doesn't she?" Uncle Gabe says.

"She sure does."

Nana has said that a few times, but I don't see it. My hair is more the color of corn than caramel, and it's wavy, when Mom's is straight. Mom's eyes are blue and mine are brown. But I feel too shy to press them for more details.

Carlton comes down off the porch. "I can't talk for long, sadly. I'm cooking dinner and then I have to pick up Mom from her Italian conversation group, but what are you doing in town, Gabe?"

"What are *you* doing?" my uncle says back. "Didn't we all swear we were never going to come back here after we graduated?"

"I'm helping out for a few weeks because Mom had a health scare—no, it's okay now, but she needed someone around. Dad died a few years ago, and my sister has three kids, so I came east for a while."

"Oh, sorry to hear that. My mom broke her knee."

Off they go, doing their adult talking thing.

Then I hear Carlton say, "What's Mia been up to?" and I tune back in.

"No idea," my uncle says. He sounds firm. Like someone has asked for something they are *not* going to get. "I haven't seen her or heard from her in years. Neither has Mom, as far as I know. Have you?" He sounds hesitant when he says that. Like he's not sure he wants to hear the answer.

Carlton shakes his head. "We had a big fight and she ghosted me. Right before she got arrested. She was burning a lot of bridges back then."

"Mia was always burning a lot of bridges," my uncle says.

Okay, so now you know. That's how I ended up staying with Nana permanently.

Mom got arrested with a backpack full of marijuana she was taking from one place to another, and she ended up spending three years in jail. Nana sued for custody of me then, and Mom gave me up.

She gave me up.

I don't know much more about it, because this is one of the things Nana never wants to talk about. "When you're older," she used to say sometimes. But it seemed like I was never old enough, and finally I gave up asking.

But now Uncle Gabe is here.

Maybe I can ask him.

"Possession with intent to distribute." Uncle Gabe shakes his head. "Even my sister couldn't sweet-talk herself out of trouble that big."

Carlton and my uncle laugh the kind of laughter adults laugh when they're talking about something that really isn't funny.

Carlton smooths down his mustache. "I used to see her a lot when Franny was little—"

Huh?

"I even babysat Franny when I was living up in Boston—"

What?!

"Those people Mia was hanging around with by then, I knew they were trouble. I tried telling her, but—"

Uncle Gabe flaps a hand. "She never listened to anyone when she was in that mode. We were all morons and she was the brilliant person with the great plan. Listen, Carlton, we ought to get going, but I think we're having a little party this Saturday. You want to come over?"

Carlton shakes his head. "I'd love to, but it's my cousin's birthday and there's a big family dinner. And I was never your mom's favorite person, Gabe."

"She had to blame someone for all that trouble Mia got into. Well, look, I'm going to be around anyway, so let's get together again and finish catching up."

Their phones beep while they send each other their phone numbers.

"Uncle Gabe," I whisper. "Uncle Gabe."

"What is it?"

"Could I, uh, get together with Carlton too?" They both look at me. "I mean, he knew Mom. And me when I was little!"

A light dawns on my uncle's face. "I'll try to make that happen."

And then Uncle Gabe is herding me over to the car and we're driving away.

I wasn't even finished looking at the house!

"Why did Nana sell this house instead of staying here?" I ask my uncle in the car.

"Houses are a lot of work to keep up, and after Pops died, there wasn't anyone around to help with that. Your mom was gone by then, and so was I, and to be honest . . . " Uncle Gabe's mouth is turned down, his forehead wrinkled. All of a sudden, I can see my nana in him. "There were a lot of good memories in this house, but there were a lot of bad memories too."

"Do you remember an apartment in Somerville where Mom and I lived? Nana said Poppy called it 'the groundhog den.'"

"Oh, that place. I heard about it. You weren't there for very long. You got some stubborn cough and Pops was back up there like a shot, putting down first and last on a nicer apartment with 'better air,' he called it." Uncle Gabe's frown gets deeper.

"I'm in college, busting my butt between classes and working in the dining hall and cleaning offices on the weekends. And your mom is getting moved into a nice apartment in Somerville. She didn't even have to pack her own boxes. Pops did that for her too."

Maybe this isn't the right time to ask him any more about Mom.

CHAPTER 11

A PHONE? WELL, THANK YOU."

That's all Nana says.

About her super-nice top-of-the-line new phone.

"I figured it would make up for some of those missed birthdays and Christmases," Uncle Gabe says.

Nana gives a little shrug.

Uncle Gabe raises his eyebrows and clicks his tongue. Once. It's the same thing Nana does when she's really annoyed but doesn't want to say anything about it. He goes back to the stove, where a pan of sauce is spreading good smells of tomatoes and garlic all through our house.

Nana looks at the box in her hands. "Franny, do me a favor and put this on the bureau in my bedroom."

Uncle Gabe says, "Ma, come on. You can do that yourself. You're supposed to stay more active."

Nana gives him a look that could freeze the entire Amazon River from Peru to the Atlantic Ocean. "This wheelchair is very unwieldy, Gabriel. You wouldn't know that, because you've never spent any time in one, let alone had an extended leg."

"You're right. But I know the more you use anything, the easier it gets. Like computers. Or wheelchairs. Or new phones!"

Nana rolls over to the side table in the living room and puts the phone down there. I know I'll be delivering it to her bedroom later, no matter what my uncle says.

Uncle Gabe goes on talking. "And you know what, I think Franny should have my old phone."

"No twelve-year-old needs a cell phone," Nana says firmly.

I've heard her say this plenty of times, and I've gotten used to the idea that I'm just going to be one of those middle-school losers with no phone, but now it's personal. I could go to school with a phone tomorrow, like Ruben and Lucy. It's like having your favorite candy bar sitting out in front of you and some adult saying you can't touch it. It's so not fair!

"Nana—" I start.

"Shush."

Uncle Gabe says, "Ma, think about it. It makes communication a lot easier. You and Franny could text, she could let you know when she was running late, you could send her reminders—"

I can tell this is sinking in a little.

"I'll think about it," she says grudgingly. Like Uncle Gabe's given her a hard problem to solve in math. "We've managed just fine up till now."

"Uh, not really," I say. "Ruben has a phone, and what his parents do is—"

"Franny, zip it!" Nana says.

"That's rude," I mutter.

Uncle Gabe drops a glob of butter into the tomato sauce, then turns the burner off underneath it. He's taken the strainer of cooked rigatoni out of the sink and now he's putting the pasta into the big pan with the cooked sauce. Droplets of tomato sauce fly everywhere, but I can tell Uncle Gabe doesn't care. I come closer to watch him stir the sauce and pasta together.

"Uncle Gabe, why are you cooking the pasta twice?"

"It picks up a better flavor this way. You finish cooking the pasta in the sauce."

"It's going to be overdone" is Nana's contribution.

Uncle Gabe ignores this and keeps talking to me. "Wait till you taste it. This is how a lot of people make pasta in Italy."

"Must be nice going to Italy on a vacation," my nana remarks. Her tone does not match this peaceful sentence.

"What's stopping you, Ma?" Now it's Uncle Gabe's turn to freeze the entire Amazon River with a few words. "You want to go to Italy? Get online and make some reservations. I bet Franny would love to go."

Of course I'd love to go to Italy.

I'd love to go to the Poconos, let alone Italy.

I set the table and we finally sit down to eat.

"I hope the delivery guys don't get here while we're eating." Uncle Gabe takes the grater and Parmesan and grates a flurry of cheese over his plate.

"Delivery people?" Nana forks up a little pasta, like she's worried it might be poisoned, and chews. I can tell she thinks it's good, but also that she doesn't want to admit this.

"Oh, we're getting a new TV. They had flat-screens on sale. I got a good deal. Ninety-day unconditional guarantee, too."

Nana puts down her fork. "A TV?"

"A new TV. Aren't you tired of that one over there?" Uncle Gabe points with his fork at Mr. Tan's TV in the corner. "It must be thirty years old."

"It still works." It's the same thing Nana says about the TV back in our apartment.

"Well, maybe it ought to take a hint from those people who retire after thirty years. It can do whatever old TVs do. Move to Florida. Write its memoirs."

"We can't just replace Mr. Tan's TV. This isn't our house."

"I'll put the old one in your bedroom. Ma, come on, be reasonable. I'm trying to do something nice for you."

"No, you're not," my nana says. "You're doing something nice for yourself and pretending it's for me. The old TV is fine. It stays where it is."

The doorbell rings.

"You go out there and tell them to take that one away."

"Nana!" I hear myself say. Why does she have to ruin everything? Mr. Tan's TV is the worst! It's like watching every show through a snowstorm!

Uncle Gabe puts down his napkin. "I'll be right back," he says. To me. I'm pretty sure he's not talking to Nana right now. He steps outside and closes the door.

Nana sighs. "Eat," she says to me, and points to my plate of food.

I will just add here that whenever I point at anything, Nana tells me it's impolite, but I guess she's allowed to do it whenever she wants.

I start eating again. What can I do? Anyway, I'm starving.

I hear the faraway rumble of the garage door opening.

In a few minutes, Nana says, "I wonder what's going on out there. I didn't hear the truck leave. Did you?"

I shake my head. My mouth is full.

"Do me a favor and take a look. What is your uncle doing out there?"

Feeling sneaky and a little ridiculous, I peek around the drapes. "The truck is still there."

The garage door rumbles again.

"Why is the truck still there?" my nana demands, like I would know.

"I don't know, but here come the guys. They look like they're coming up from the driveway."

"Huh." Nana forgets she doesn't like Uncle Gabe's cooking and has a bite of pasta. "Maybe one of them needed to use the bathroom, and your uncle let them into the basement."

"I didn't hear the toilet flush," I say. "Uncle Gabe is coming up. I can hear him on the stairs."

"Come here! Quick, sit!"

Uncle Gabe sits back down at the table and picks up his fork.

Nana clears her throat. "I'm sorry your rigatoni must be cold by now, Gabriel."

"It's fine," my uncle says.

"Franny could put it in the microwave for you."

"It's fine," he repeats.

There is an awkward silence. A few more minutes of this and we'll be turning on NPR and listening to the news.

"Were the guys okay about having to take back the TV?" Nana asks. "I hope they weren't too angry."

"They didn't take the TV back."

I drop my fork and it rings onto my plate, but Nana doesn't tell me to be careful or remind me this is a rental and the china belongs to someone else. She says, "What?"

"They didn't take the TV back."

"What do you mean? Where is it? They didn't just leave it in the yard or something."

"It's in my room downstairs." Uncle Gabe wipes his mouth. "Just because you want to watch that crappy old TV doesn't mean I have to."

I would laugh, but I know better than to let one sound escape. I make a choking noise and press my napkin to my mouth. Uncle Gabe steals a look at me and winks.

"What am I supposed to do with that thing when you go back to Wisconsin in two months?" Nana says.

"Ma, if you don't want it, leave it there. I doubt the people renting you this house are going to complain about a brand-new flat-screen TV in their basement. I doubt that very seriously."

Nana looks furious but says nothing more. The rest of dinner is conducted in silence.

After I finish my homework, I sneak down to Uncle Gabe's room and we watch hockey together. The new TV totally kicks butt. I can see practically every hair in the goalie's nose.

THE NEXT DAY AFTER school, I'm fixing myself some crackers and cheese in the kitchen with the phone clamped under my chin, listening to Lucy complain. We're rushing to catch up before it's time for Lucy to put her phone away. Here in New Jersey I'm just fixing my after-school snack, but in London, Lucy's already had dinner and done her homework.

Lucy's gran is driving her wild. Now she's insisting that Lucy use a metronome whenever she practices the piano. And then,

Lucy says, her gran stands in the dining room during the whole practice session to make sure Lucy doesn't turn the metronome back off.

"And *every time* I make a mistake, she tsks," Lucy tells me. "It's tsk, tsk, tsk the *entire* half hour. It's like having *two* metronomes going! And then Gran says to Mum, 'Lucy doesn't seem to be making very brilliant progress with her piano.'"

"That bites," I say absentmindedly.

Lucy can tell I don't have my head in this discussion. "What's going on with you?"

I look around although I know Nana is taking a nap and Uncle Gabe is downstairs working. "I saw the house where my mom grew up."

"You never saw it before?"

"No. Never." Which is weird, when I stop and think about it, because Uncle Gabe was right about the distance. It isn't that far away from where we live now. An easy drive, even for Nana, who always takes Route 10 instead of I-80.

"What was it like?"

"Well, it's a nice big house, with a big yard. . . . There was a trampoline and swing set, and a garden with a fence. . . . It's a lot nicer than our apartment."

Lucy waits to make sure I'm done.

"It was just weird seeing where Mom lived for so many years. I saw her windows. But no one was home, so we couldn't go in.

And then my uncle said something about how it wasn't really all that happy a place."

"Huh," Lucy says.

"I wish I had some pictures of Mom," I hear myself say. "I can hardly remember what she looks like."

"There are family pictures all *over* our house," Lucy says.

I know she doesn't mean to make me feel bad. "Ruben's, too. I don't even know what I looked like when I was a baby."

"Maybe you should ask your nana if she has any scrapbooks."

"Scrapbooks?"

"Or photo albums. Back before smartphones, when people used to get their film developed, a lot of them would organize the pictures into these big scrapbooks. Maybe your nana has some of those. That's what Gran has."

"Maybe," I say.

"Can't hurt to ask," Lucy offers, sounding cheerful.

Which just goes to show Lucy doesn't always know what she's talking about. Sometimes it can hurt to ask if no one wants to answer your questions.

CHAPTER 12

I DECIDE TO MAKE A pecan pie for the party on Saturday. Uncle Gabe says it's his favorite kind of pie because his ex-girlfriend, Mely, made it for their first Thanksgiving together.

It seems like a good way to make him feel welcome. Like we appreciate him. And I want to show him I have some kitchen flair, like he has.

When I tell Nana, she gives an irritated sigh. "Just make some brownies. I'll have Gabe pick up a few boxes of mix for you. That's more like your skill set right now."

I make up my mind to just ignore her. I don't know what's with her lately. You'd think she'd be happier, with Uncle Gabe around to help, but that hasn't worked out the way I thought.

Dr. Yao makes a really good pecan pie with maple syrup in it, and Ruben gets me her recipe.

"It's easy," he tells me while I look it over. He printed it out and scribbled some words in the margins. "I've helped her make it. Just don't forget the cinnamon."

The only thing I'm doing different from Dr. Yao is I'm using a frozen pie crust. I've never made a pie crust before and another piece of advice from Nana was not to try to make my first pie crust on the day of the party. I decided that was good advice.

On Saturday morning everything goes great. I remember to prebake the pie crust in the oven, which is what I was worried about forgetting. Once it's out, I tumble the pecans inside, whisk the filling all together, and pour it over. Then I put the pie in the oven with only a little slopping and I go take a shower before Uncle Gabe gets up and uses all the hot water.

The rest of the morning goes fast, with stuff like putting away Nana's magazines and running the vacuum cleaner. In the middle of my housework, I hear some banging on the stairs. Uncle Gabe comes up from the basement with a card table. I go to help him. It doesn't look heavy, but it's awkward. Then I help him carry up folding chairs. There are eight of them in the basement. We put four around the card table in my bedroom and four out in the living room for extra seats. Then it's time to find a cloth and wipe the furniture down, because it's so dirty that the dust hangs in long streamers that make me think of rabbit fur.

"What in the world is the card table for?" Nana scowls from what has become her permanent seat on the sofa. I think she's nervous about the party.

"I thought maybe the kids could play some games in Franny's room if they got bored."

"Games?" my grandmother asks. "People come, they eat, they chat for a bit, and then they leave. Are people going to be hanging around here all afternoon?"

"They might." Uncle Gabe sounds very serious. But then he winks at me.

"Besides, we don't have any games," Nana argues.

"Yes, we do," Uncle Gabe says. "There's a whole shelf of them down in the basement."

The games are mostly old-fashioned ones like Chinese checkers and Yahtzee, but I also see Gyrating Hamsters and Munchkin, which are some of my favorites. I just wish Ruben wanted to play them more often. He's more into the heavy strategy games.

Uncle Gabe's other major contributions to the party are a case of Bass Ale and a gallon jug of white wine.

"It's barely one o'clock!" Nana wheels into the bathroom, scowling. A few minutes later she is yelling for me.

If the toilet has to clog, it's better for it to clog before the guests get here.

BY TWO O'CLOCK EVERYONE has showed up and our house is full. There are people everywhere and I think they're all having a pretty good time.

The adults are out in the living room, standing around drinking and eating and talking. Nana found an Eddie Palmieri album in Mr. Tan's collection, which goes to show he has good taste in music, and it's spinning. (Mom's stereo is still safe in the basement.) A few younger kids are running around where their parents can watch them.

Reyna is in Nana's bedroom, sitting on the floor with Dr. Morgenstern's kids. (Dr. Morgenstern showed up after all!)

In my bedroom, Ruben, Eliot, Arun, and I are playing Munchkin. Arun and Ruben are fighting it out the whole game, but at the end Eliot has amazing luck. He gets the Chainsaw of Bloody Dismemberment and the Pantyhose of Giant Strength and then it turns out he has a Doppelganger card in his hand for the last fight. That doubles his strength, and he wins the game. He raises his hands over his head, cheering for himself. I'm happy for him. Eliot shows up for Game Day every week and almost never wins, no matter what we play, and he's always a good sport about it, which isn't easy.

Those last-minute changes are one of my favorite things about Munchkin. You have no idea who's going to win until the last few hands.

It's one of Ruben's *least* favorite things about Munchkin.

Before Ruben can drag everyone into another round to get his revenge, I say, "Let's have some dessert!"

Out in the living room, the adults must have had the same thought, because half the tres leches cake is gone and there has been some serious damage done to the cookie platter. But my pie is still in one piece. They must have been waiting for me. I go right over and pick up the pie server.

"Franny—" my nana says as I cut into the pie.

There's something wrong with it. The pie server skids right over its browned top. I try again. Maybe there's something wrong with this pie server. It can't chop through the pecans. I try sliding the pie server under the crust. That's when I find out the crust is totally glued to the pan.

"What's going on?" Ruben asks.

"I can't get the pie out," I mutter to him.

"Can't get the *pie* out?" Rubes never whispers anything. "What's wrong with it?"

I hear the terrible sound of kindly adult laughter.

Oh great. They know already!

"I had that happen with a pecan pie once," I hear Dr. Morgenstern say. "The first time I had my wife's parents over. I wanted to make something special."

"That's what Franny wanted to do," I hear Nana say. Ugh! If I weren't so busy trying to break into the pie, I'd give her the world's dirtiest look.

"The pie might be a little overdone," Dr. Yao says in her gentle voice. "Let's get a metal spoon and we can just scoop it out."

"The recipe said 'roughly forty minutes'! I gave it a few extra minutes, until it stopped jiggling—"

"Oh," Dr. Yao says.

I don't like the sound of that "oh."

"You need to take it out *while* it's still jiggling. You can remember that for next time."

Ruben says, "I wrote in 'Remove in forty minutes.'"

"You did not," I say.

"Yes, I did." He looks at me mildly. "I drew an arrow and wrote it down. I remember."

Ruben's dad waves his bottle of Bass Ale. "Ruben, buddy, we really need to work on your handwriting."

They're all smiling. They all think it's funny. Even Uncle Gabe is laughing.

Except for Nana and Aunt Gravy. Nana catches my attention with her steady gaze and presses her lips together sympathetically.

I take another deep breath, and then another one, and then I force myself to smile. I feel like my cheeks are about to crack. "Oh well!" I chirp. It's exactly what Aunt Gravy would say. Great!

I make myself put the pie server down extra carefully. Instead of throwing it, which is what I want to do. Then I walk away fast down the hall to the bathroom.

Once I'm safely inside, I glare at myself in the cloudy mirror and give a silent scream that shows all my teeth, down to the molars in the back.

Then I sit on the toilet and just let myself feel like the dumbest person in the world for a while.

I mean, one kid from our school was on *MasterChef Junior* a few years ago.

But me? I can't even make a stupid pie.

Nana was right. I should have made brownies from a box mix instead.

I hate when Nana is right.

I get up and wash my face and then look at myself. My face isn't too pink. One of the worst things about me is that when I get angry or upset, my face and neck get pink.

But I'm kind of back to my normal color now. So I think it's okay to go back out. I can't stay in here forever.

Out in the living room, the adults are into their conversations again.

Dr. Yao calls me over. She's making the pecan pie into parfaits. She's just scooped the pie filling into water glasses, added the vanilla ice cream that was supposed to go on top, and finished them off with some spray whipped cream.

I peer into the pie tin. The crust is still there, glued down firmly, but all the insides are out.

"And we don't have to soak it. We can just throw the pie pan away."

"I feel stupid," I say quietly.

Dr. Yao puts her hand on my shoulder. "You should have been there the first time I made lechón. I wanted to make sure it was done. And, oh my goodness, was it *done*! It was like eating a shoe!" She hands me a parfait.

The parfait is just as good as the pie would have been. Maybe better, because it has ice cream *and* whipped cream on it. Eating it cheers me up.

～

THE YAOS LEAVE FIRST. They have another party to go to, Dr. Yao says. Then Aunt Gravy and Dr. Morgenstern and Nana's office friends.

Arun and Eliot stay for a while longer because we've decided to play Yahtzee. If it's too cringe, we'll just stop. But it ends up being okay. Old-fashioned but still fun.

"We should play Mafia sometime," Arun says.

We've finished our game and Eliot's putting everything away neatly in Mr. Tan's dusty old Yahtzee box with the taped-up corners. Eliot is what Nana calls meticulous. You should see the inside of his school locker. Everything in its place. You'd never find an old banana skin or crunched-up homework paper at the bottom. Funny, Arun is just the opposite. When he opens his locker, six different things fall out.

"You can just play it with a pack of cards. Vijay taught me." Vijay is Arun's oldest brother.

"I like playing cards," I say. Card games are not Ruben's favorite, so we almost never play them at his house.

"I bet we're not going to be playing Munchkin tomorrow," Eliot says in his low-key way. Arun gives a snort of laughter. I think it's the closest any of us would come to mentioning the fact that Ruben isn't the greatest sport when he loses. Rubes can't help it. He just hates losing so much.

"Is Tate going to be there, you think? How was it last week?" I ask them.

"Pretty much what I expected," Eliot says. "Tate did a lot of trash-talking and at the end he tried to bust out some obscure rule none of us had heard of that would give him an extra point—Ruben shut him down, though."

"Bro, you're the one who told Ruben about him," Arun says.

"Well, I didn't know Tate was going to become a permanent fixture."

"Maybe Tate won't be there tomorrow," I say.

We all three trade looks. You never know what other people are thinking, but I'm pretty sure that we're all silently agreeing that of course Tate will be there tomorrow. We can all tell Ruben thinks he's the greatest.

"Let me go say goodbye to your grandmother. Mom said, 'Make *sure* you thank Franny's grandma for the party.'" Eliot rolls his eyes, and Arun and I do too in solidarity.

"It must be weird being in a wheelchair," Arun says.

I nod. "Nana says she never feels comfortable in it."

"But she's going to be okay, right, Franny?"

"Of course," I say. But inside me, a little snake of doubt wakes up and starts wiggling around. Great—another item for Things Currently Worrying Franny Petroski.

CHAPTER 13

WHAT A MESS IN here. Someone's going to have to deal with this."

Nana says "someone" in an accusing way, like she's going to be the one collecting all the crumpled-up napkins and half-eaten parfaits. I feel a flash of irritation. I think I've been pretty good about helping out since Nana got hurt.

"That party was fun," I tell her. "We should have one again next weekend."

Nana does the half laugh she gives sometimes when she's tired. "Uh, no."

"Didn't you have a good time?" I ask.

"It was all right. I was getting pretty tired by the time your friends left. I'm going to go rest for a little bit. Can you do some cleaning up?"

I watch Nana roll down the hall toward her room.

Sometimes I wonder if it would actually kill Nana to admit she enjoyed something.

Ugh.

It's not that bad cleaning up, because we mostly used

disposable plates, cups, and napkins. Nana usually never uses them, but she says when you have a broken knee, there's an excuse. Besides, we didn't have enough real dishes for everyone. I gather up the disposable stuff and throw it away, and then I go through the house collecting the real plates and glasses and take them into the kitchen.

I load the dishwasher and start washing what's left. I'm done with the plates and almost done with the glasses when Uncle Gabe comes up from the basement.

"You're not using the dishwasher?" he asks.

"It's already full," I tell him.

He sits at the kitchen table to keep me company, I guess.

"Did *you* have fun at the party?" I ask him.

"Sure. It was cool. It was nice of you to get it organized for me. When's the last time you two had a party?"

"We had birthday parties when I was little." Although those birthday parties were usually me, Ruben, and Lucy and maybe one or two other kids. "And then, you know, I kind of outgrew them."

Although I'm not sure why that would happen. I guess it depends on the family. I mean, Ruben still has a birthday party every year.

"Maybe your nana has dinner parties instead?" my uncle suggests.

I have to laugh imagining Nana throwing a dinner party.

I mean, aside from the food, where would everyone sit in our apartment?

"Was Nana always the way she is now?" I ask.

"What do you mean?"

I remember Nana rolling away from me into her room earlier. "Everything is too much trouble or too expensive or makes too much mess or is too noisy . . . "

"Cranky, you mean? Negative?" My uncle sighs. "No. She wasn't always this way. When your mom and I were little, our parents had parties sometimes. And they loved having people over to play cards. I remember they used to laugh so hard downstairs! Listening to them laugh was the best way to fall asleep. Your nana was a real card shark. The euchre queen."

I didn't know Nana liked card games, the way I do. "Shut up!"

Uncle Gabe laughs. "You shut up! She was younger then, and I think things hadn't, well, piled up on her the way they did later. Your mom—"

Uh-oh.

"She had a way of wearing people down. I know you probably get tired of hearing that."

Nana never talks about Mom enough for me to get tired of it.

"Take the pecan pie incident," my uncle goes on. "I saw you take a deep breath and go away and get yourself calmed down. Well, a lot of the time, your mom couldn't do that. If she lost her temper, it was like watching the *Hindenburg* catch fire. All you could do was wait for it to explode. There wasn't any way to stop it."

I thought I wanted him to talk about Mom, but now I'm not so sure. "Well, maybe it's just that she wasn't a big fake like everybody else, always pretending things were great when they weren't."

Uncle Gabe's brow crinkles. "Do you remember her saying that?"

"No."

"Because that's pretty much exactly what your mother would say whenever someone would talk to her about staying calm."

I don't know what to think about that. I store it away for later.

"Uncle Gabe? Do you think Mom's okay, wherever she is?"

My uncle gets up from the table and pushes his chair in. "I hope so. I mean, there's no reason to think otherwise."

"You don't think she's dead. Or anything," I rush to add, just in case he thinks I'm a terrible person to wonder about that.

"I don't know, Franny. There's no way for me to know. I hope not." He pats me on the arm. "I'm pretty sure your nana would hear about it if something like that happened."

His fingers are really cold. All of a sudden I feel fear leap up, the same fear I felt when I found Nana on the sidewalk in front of our apartment.

"YOU TOLD HER YOU don't *know*?!" Nana shouts from the living room.

This argument is my fault.

When Uncle Gabe and I finished talking about Mom, I went to find Nana in her bedroom. I woke her up from her nap and asked her whether Mom was dead.

Nana sat up, rubbed her eyes, and then ran her fingers through her hair. It's like she *wants* her hair standing straight up from her head. She blinked hard. Then she told me she was sure Mom wasn't.

"How do you know?" I asked.

"I just do. A mom knows. Can you help me get back into this thing?"

I went over to hold the wheelchair while Nana got herself into it. "Do you know where Mom is?" I asked.

"Frances, I swear to holy God, I have no idea where your mom is right now."

Nana is not much for church, but I know she wouldn't swear to holy God if she were lying. So that helped me calm down at least a little.

She patted my arm, rolled down the hall into the living room, and started yelling at Uncle Gabe, who was making himself a bowl of potato chips and dip in the kitchen.

I retreated into my room—but that doesn't mean I can't hear everything. Not the way they're yelling.

"I didn't know what to say!" my uncle says. "Do you want me to *lie* to her?"

"I want you to talk appropriately to a twelve-year-old girl! She doesn't need to be thinking about all that! You come in here, stirring everything up and making her talk about stuff that hasn't been an issue for years!"

"Maybe she should be talking about it, Ma!"

"Oh, so now you're a therapist!"

"Look, I never asked for all this! I never claimed to be an expert in child psychology!"

"*That* much is obvious!"

"Fine," Uncle Gabe says. "Fine! I knew this was going to be a disaster."

I hear the crunch of a chip bag getting squashed. Then heavy footsteps coming down the hall. And the sound of the basement door banging shut.

I take a few deep breaths. Then I come out from my room.

The chip bag is lying all balled up on the kitchen floor. Nana is sitting in front of the TV in her wheelchair, her forehead scrunched up. Just like Uncle Gabe's got when I asked him about Mom.

"Nana? Do you, um, want the remote?"

She sighs. "Yes, please."

"Do you want to get on the sofa?"

"If you move the coffee table, I can do it," Nana says. "The people in my knee injury support group are on me to become more active."

We moved the furniture around for the party. I shove the coffee table back away from the sofa against the wall, where it's out of Nana's way.

"Thank you. And could you throw away that potato chip bag?"

I get Nana the remote and pick up the bag. I empty the rest of the crushed chips into my mouth and then, the way I always do, I stop and consider the bag. It's a nice shiny dark green, and I like the way it crinkles. Inside the bag is silvery. It looks like it would be easy to wash clean—I bet it would be cool for some project—

"Franny," my nana says. "Don't you even *think* about holding on to that greasy, nasty old bag! Put it in the garbage and go finish your homework or read a book or draw or something."

"Fine!" I hear myself yell.

I throw it into the garbage and stomp away down the hall to my room. The exact same thing Uncle Gabe did.

We are the worst family ever. We can't even have a party without getting in a fight.

UNCLE GABE ISN'T THE one who got me thinking about Mom. He got me talking about Mom. There's a difference.

There wasn't that much point in talking about Mom before Uncle Gabe came here.

Nana doesn't like to talk about Mom, and Mr. Burns can't talk about her because he never knew her. He can only listen to me talk about her.

No one else where we live now knew my mom either.

Maybe that's the real reason Nana moved out here from Livingston.

Try googling "Mia Petroski." Go ahead, give it a try.

In case you're interested, the last name Petroski is the 106,088th most common last name in the world. Yao is the 91st. Bernal is 1,138th.

My point is that it's not like there are a lot of people named "Mia Petroski" out there.

The last time I looked, there was a college student in Columbia, Missouri; a realtor in Orlando, Florida; and a gastroenterologist in Pierre, South Dakota. None of them are Mom. They all have pictures on their profiles, so I know. Another Mia Petroski died last year, but she was ninety-five years old. Not Mom either.

I might not talk about Mom all that much.

But I think about Mom a lot more than I talk. Especially now that Uncle Gabe's face reminds me of her every day.

Maybe I always did think about her more than I wanted to admit. Even to myself. Especially to myself.

CHAPTER 14

DO PEOPLE IN YOUR family ever fight?" I ask Ruben at lunchtime on Monday.

We're alone at our table because everyone else is still in the lunch line.

"Sure. All the time." Ruben sniffs his forkful of noodles and then stuffs in a huge mouthful and talks through them. "Want some? It's veggie."

He pushes a mound onto my plate, next to my sad grilled cheese and carrot sticks.

"How come?" he wants to know.

"Oh, my nana and my uncle had a dumb fight after the party on Saturday." I leave out my argument with Nana about the potato chip bag.

"Right now my parents are arguing about where my sister should apply to college. Dad wants all top colleges, Mom says they need plenty of safety schools, and Reyna wants one of those big party colleges out in the Midwest that have huge football games and keggers. They both get mad at her whenever she says that."

Eliot, Arun, and Tate materialize at the same time, bang down their trays, and sit. Ruben turns to them. "Hey, guys, do people in your families argue?"

Wait a moment, I want to say. I don't mind asking Eliot and Arun, but Tate is another story. I don't want him in my business.

"Who wants to know?" Arun asks.

"Uh, my uncle and my nana had a big fight over the weekend." I shrug, like it's no big deal.

"*My* parents don't fight," Tate says.

Of course they don't, I say in my head.

Tate goes on, "They both say they're capable of having reasonable discussions."

"My parents never fight in front of me," Arun says. "But I can always tell when they're mad at each other."

"My mom and stepdad don't fight that often," Eliot says, "and neither do my dad and stepmom, but my stepsisters are *at* each other, people! I didn't know twins could be like that! Hazel *bit* Heidi last time I was over there." He slurps some milk. "Oh, hey, Franny, I think I left my hat when I was at your house on Saturday. Could you check? It's a 'Ski Wyoming' hat."

"Oh, I remember putting it in the closet. I'll bring it tomorrow."

"That party at Franny's?" Tate grins. "I heard there was a delicious pecan-and-glue pie."

There's a frozen moment of silence before Ruben starts laughing. "Franny got the recipe wrong."

See, this is one of the things about Ruben. As far as he's concerned, the pecan pie incident is just something funny that happened. He doesn't always stop to think about how I might feel about it.

He adds, thoughtfully, "Hot maple syrup *is* kind of like glue. That's what my mom said in the car afterward."

Ruben, shut up, I say in my head. Thank God not out loud.

Arun clears his throat. "Actually, bro, the pie was really good."

Tate laughs. "Oh right."

I look at him. "I guess it was one of those things where you just had to be there."

That shuts Tate up.

IT'S NICE TO GET home and have the house smell like food— and not TV dinners, either. The table is already set too. Uncle Gabe is standing at the counter, his phone to his ear. He nods at me and I nod back.

Nana is settled on the sofa with our laptop next to her, busy with her new phone. She stares for a long moment, types, then waits again. "Darn," she says.

"What are you doing, Nana?"

She holds up her phone. "I'm refreshing my Spanish. How was school?"

I stop in the middle of unwinding my scarf. Lucy made it for me in all my favorite colors. She calls it my Doctor Who scarf. But it does take a while to take off because it's really long. "Spanish?"

Nana looks a little embarrassed, like I've caught her doing something she should be ashamed of. "I need to do something while I'm sitting around all day, and it turns out there are all kinds of iPhone apps that help you learn new languages. I took Spanish in high school, but now I'm rusty. It would be useful if we had another person in the office who could speak some Spanish. Karen can't be there all the time."

"How do you say 'dental plaque' in Spanish?" I ask.

"Give me a second. 'Placa dental.' What is it in French?"

"'Plaque dentaire,'" I tell her. Nana laughs, so I confess a secret. "Sometimes I call this house La Maison de la Plaque Dentaire. Just to myself. Because it's the color of dental plaque."

Nana's face splits into a grin. "You're absolutely right! But maybe we should call it La casa de placa dental."

"Either sounds so much better than Dental Plaque House," Uncle Gabe says, shoving his phone into his pocket and checking on something in the oven. "Five more minutes. Now come on, Ma—stop teasing her."

Nana puts down her phone. She digs into the pocket on the side of her wheelchair and holds something out to me.

It's flat.

It's rectangular.

It's a smartphone.

I think Nana is *giving* it to me.

My grandmother starts to laugh. "She can't believe it."

"It's my old phone," Uncle Gabe says. "I thought you probably didn't want your nana's old flip phone. Unless you want to dial up a mastodon, that thing wouldn't be much use."

"Now, Gabe, that phone still works just fine." Nana looks back at me. "This is against my better judgment, and it might be temporary. I'm not promising you can keep this phone forever, but your uncle is right about one thing—"

Behind her, Uncle Gabe lets his jaw drop in disbelief and I bite my lip not to laugh.

"—things aren't exactly normal right now. Sometimes I need to get ahold of you. And from now on, when you're running late, you text me. Deal?"

I can barely believe the words *you text me* have come out of my nana's mouth.

"Deal!" I turn the phone over. I'm going to buy a dope new cover for it. No, I'm going to cover the whole back with stickers—

I can hear Nana go on talking, something about giving her the phone by nine o'clock every night and how she's going to have total access to all my accounts—all the adult stuff I would have expected—but I'm so excited, I can't even pay attention.

I soon find out that one of the phone rules is that I'm not allowed to have it at the table during meals. Uncle Gabe is allowed to have his. Unfair.

"Your uncle needs his for work," Nana tells me.

Uncle Gabe puts a spoonful of baked ziti on my plate. "Also, I am no longer twelve years old and I get to decide for myself whether I have my phone at the table."

Nana presses her lips together and reaches for her fork.

Uncle Gabe sneaks another look at his phone. Then he clicks it off and slides it into his back pocket and says, "Franny, what do you think about going down to the shore this weekend?"

"In January?" Nana says.

I could have told you she was going to say that.

"The beach in the winter is great! The boardwalk is still there, and it's way less crowded. And I am not leaving New Jersey without going down to Asbury Park—that was one of my favorite places to hang out when I was in high school. We can take a long walk along the boardwalk and grab something to eat at one of the restaurants down there—"

"They'll all be closed," Nana jabs in.

"—play some pinball, walk by the Stone Pony, check out Convention Hall. Why don't you see if one of your friends wants to come along?"

"Seriously?" I say. Ruben will never believe I'm asking him to go somewhere. It's always the other way around. "Dope!"

Nana clears her throat.

I look at her. I know she was waiting for me to do that,

because she raises her eyebrows. It takes me a little while longer to figure out what she wants me to do next. "Nana, is it okay if I go?"

"Thank you for asking." Nana says this in a way I would describe as "ominously polite." "Yes, as long as your chores and homework get taken care of beforehand. I don't want any homework surprises on Sunday. Capeesh?"

"Yes," I say flatly. Trust Nana to take all the fun out of it that she can.

When we're done eating, I clear the table quickly so Uncle Gabe and I have time for a walk before it gets too late. Uncle Gabe tries to take a walk every day. It's usually after lunch, but sometimes he has calls and then he walks after dinner. Nana always says I can go. She thinks the exercise is good for me. It's fun walking around town in the dark, with the streets so quiet and the lights from people's windows shining out onto the snow.

A FEW DAYS LATER I manage to catch Ruben alone in the cafeteria before school starts.

Lately Tate is attached to Ruben all the time. But Tate takes the bus to school and Ruben walks, so sometimes I can find Ruben on his own before the buses come in. It's annoying I have to think about that now, but whatever. I ask him about going to the beach.

Ruben actually puts down his bagel. "*You're* going to the beach?"

His surprise isn't super flattering, but I get it. Nana and I almost never go anywhere. And if we did, it would never occur to her to ask one of my friends along. She's always embarrassed by her nervous driving, the way she'll drive around the block to avoid a tricky left turn, the way she's always the slowest driver on the parkway.

"My uncle is taking me. On Saturday. Can you come?"

"Sorry, Franny. Tate and I are going to a chess clinic down in Princeton that day."

"Oh." I nod.

"Dad is driving us. He's so happy I'm getting more serious about chess, he's taking us out to dinner after the clinic. He says he likes to see me making better use of my time."

I wonder whether "hanging out with Franny" counts as a good use of Ruben's time. "Cool."

"Hey, how's it going with your nana and uncle and everything?"

"I like having my uncle around. We go out and do stuff, he buys me things, he cooks all these tasty dinners, we watch hockey together—"

Ruben nods enthusiastically. "Like I've told you, aunts and uncles are the greatest! I just wish you had more of them."

There's an awkward pause.

I fiddle with one of the patches on my backpack like I can smooth away the bumpy stitches. I'm not going to lie. There are times I wish Ruben would get a clue. Maybe figure out that I get tired of being reminded how great his family is. Especially in comparison to mine.

And you know something? Nana and I don't do so badly anyway. Especially with Uncle Gabe around.

"That sounded kind of obnoxious. Sorry," Ruben adds. One good thing about Ruben. If he thinks he's done something wrong, he'll admit it straight up.

"No worries," I tell him. That's one of Lucy's expressions.

He nods and shoves the rest of his bagel into his mouth.

It's nice just sitting here with Ruben, even when he does come out with one of his blunders. Ruben Yao is my oldest best friend. Tate is annoying, but he doesn't change that. Sometimes I feel like nothing will ever change it. This is one of those moments.

Just like his parents, Ruben is a good person.

I trust him.

He's such an open book. I can't be like Ruben about everything, because my life is so different from his. But maybe it wouldn't hurt to riffle the pages of my own book a little more. Let the people I like catch some glimpses of what's written in there.

There's some stuff I've been keeping to myself for a long time. And it weighs me down.

"Rubes, you want to know something?"

"Sure."

"It's something about my . . . uh, my mom."

"Did she finally call your nana?"

"It's the Yao-ster!" Isaiah Blanchard from the Chess Club passes by. Ruben reaches out to give him a passing high five. I cross my fingers and hope Isaiah doesn't stop to hang out. My luck holds, and he keeps walking.

"No, it's something else." I sneak a look at him. He's just waiting for me to tell him whatever it is, looking more puzzled by the moment. "My mom was, um, mentally ill."

Right away I wonder if I said that correctly. Maybe I should have said Mom "*is* mentally ill." But is she still? I don't have a clue.

"Mentally *ill*?"

Oh crap. It sounds like those two words echo from one end of the cafeteria to the other, and I look around to see if everyone is staring at us. But no one is. I'm thankful that no one who matters in our sixth-grade class cares about whatever nerdy thing Franny Petroski and Ruben Yao are discussing. I'm also wishing that Ruben could figure out how to speak in a quiet voice. "Ruben, shush!"

"But what are you talking about? Mental illness? What kind of mental illness?"

"Bipolar disorder."

"I didn't know that."

"Hardly anyone does." Really, just me and Nana. Uncle Gabe knows. And some people like judges and social workers, they know too.

"I'm not sure I even know what that is. Why didn't you tell me before? Oh!" Ruben's face clears. "Did your nana tell you not to say anything?"

It's easiest just to nod, so I do. But it's not exactly right. Like everything about Mom, it's complicated. Nana never came out and said, "Don't tell anyone." She didn't have to. I knew.

I knew because *Nana* never wanted to talk about it. She told me when I was old enough to ask why I didn't live with Mom anymore. After that, she'd only mention it if she absolutely had to. If Mom's mental illness was such a terrible thing that Nana never wanted the words in her mouth, it wasn't anything I should talk about either. I mean, Nana will talk about root canals at the dinner table until you're glad the meal is over. But she never wants to talk about bipolar disorder.

"When you're older."

"When I'm not so tired."

"Why do you want to talk about that when we're having a nice evening?"

Those are the things she says instead.

The five-minute warning bell rings. Ruben starts getting his books together. "Franny, I've got to go."

"Don't tell anyone. About my mom. Okay?"

Ruben gives a quick nod, stands up, and slings on his backpack. Then he's out the door.

BIPOLAR DISORDER IS ONE of those things I don't know much about. Nana doesn't want to talk about it, like I said, and I can't ask anyone else because they might be curious why I'm asking.

You're probably thinking, why doesn't this dumb Franny Petroski person just do an Internet search?

Well, I have, but there's so much info out there, and a lot of it is really hard to read and understand.

Googling "bipolar disorder" isn't like googling "Mia Petroski" and browsing through a few skimpy hits.

Google "bipolar disorder" and something like 230,000,000 entries pop up. Even though a lot of them say the same things using slightly different words, it's pretty easy to get overwhelmed.

Lifelong mental health condition—

Emotional highs (mania) followed by lows (depression)—

Often treated with medications and psychological counseling—

Hospitalization may be necessary to stabilize—

That kind of stuff. There's so much of it. Those are bad enough, but then there are the other things I come across.

Bipolar is the most likely psychiatric disorder to be inherited—

Scientists confirm strong genetic component—

I usually stop reading right there.

CHAPTER 15

NANA IS STILL IN her room when we leave for the beach on Saturday morning. Either sleeping in or just staying out of our way. I leave her a note on the table reminding her where we are and that there are leftovers she can nuke for lunch.

Uncle Gabe is amused by this. "Hey, brave new world. You can just text Ma now. You don't need to do notes anymore!"

It's funny to think of not writing notes to Nana. We've done it for so many years. I kind of like all the notes Nana has left me—things like *Please empty the dishwasher* or *Taking a walk with Gracie, back at six*. I started saving them a while ago. I don't know why yet. I might put them into a collage or something someday, but so far they're just piled up in a candy box. They all smell like chocolate now.

"Oh, well, we're used to doing it this way," I say, and leave it like that.

"It's too bad one of your friends couldn't come."

"Ruben was busy and Lucy's in London." It crossed my mind to ask Arun or Eliot, but they're kind of a matched set in my mind. Uncle Gabe said I could only ask one person.

I've hardly seen Ruben since I told him about Mom, and when I have, it's been him and Tate together like a grilled cheese. I wish I could catch him alone again and make sure we're okay and repeat what I said about not telling anyone about Mom. Sometimes Ruben misses things like that.

While Uncle Gabe drives, we chat. He tells me about what it's like to live in Madison. That most of the year it's beautiful and green, with lakes everywhere. That in the winter everything turns brown and white and the lakes freeze so solid everyone is out on them—playing hockey, cross-country skiing, walking their dogs, you name it. That's why Uncle Gabe learned how to ice-skate and snowshoe, so he would have reasons to get outside in the winter instead of just sitting in front of his computer. He tells me that he still hangs out mostly with a bunch of friends he made in college. And that he's dated around, but only one girl, Mely, was anything serious. They broke it off, but they're still good friends.

It sounds like the kind of life I'd like to have when I'm grown up.

Only I'm not going to be a programmer. I'm going to be an artist, like Miss Midori. So is Lucy. We're going to share an apartment and maybe have an art supply store so we're always meeting other artists, people like us. Anyway, that was our plan. Sometimes I wonder if Lucy is ever going to come back from London.

Before I start seeing any signs for the beach, Uncle Gabe takes an exit off the highway that seems familiar.

"Uncle Gabe, where are we going?"

"Oh, I asked Carlton if he wanted to come."

Huh. I thought it was just going to be me and Uncle Gabe.

"Is there a problem?" Uncle Gabe asks. "You can deal with a surprise, right? You're not like Ma?"

"Oh no," I reassure him before I have a chance to think about what I'm saying.

Of course, once Carlton is in the car, Uncle Gabe and him just talk, talk, talk. A lot about high school. A lot about their jobs. Carlton is a makeup artist in LA. That sounds pretty cool, until he says, "I thought I was going to be doing Taylor Swift, but actually now it's mostly brides."

And to hear Uncle Gabe go on and on about writing software for a big hospital system, you'd think his job was way fascinating.

First I try to pay attention and then I just sink down in the back seat and watch the cars whizzing past on the Garden State Parkway, and then I think I must fall asleep, because the next thing I know, Uncle Gabe is parking the car in front of the boardwalk.

It turns out both Uncle Gabe and Nana were right about Asbury Park in January.

Nana was right that it's cold. And that a bunch of stuff is closed. Uncle Gabe was right that Asbury Park is cool.

But the coolest part about it isn't the boardwalk or Convention Hall, which is this old redbrick building on the waterfront. It's the huge flat beach that goes a long way out to the ocean. I walk down the steps onto the sand. The wind picks up and I stop to tuck my scarf around my neck.

"Where are you going, Franny?" my uncle calls.

"I want to walk down there and look at the water," I say.

"Carlton and I are going to go in here and grab a coffee. You can meet us when you're done. You have your phone, right?"

That's the difference between Uncle Gabe and Nana. Nana would never let me wander off alone in Asbury Park. "A twelve-year-old girl alone on the boardwalk," I can hear her say. "I don't think so."

I wander down toward the water. The sand is pale tan, the ocean is dark gray and rough with big flecks of foam, and the sky over the ocean is pearly gray with patches of blue here and there. It gives me ideas for a collage or maybe a landscape made out of cloth scraps. I love cloth. It's everywhere and you can get tons of it for free and you can do all kinds of different things with it. I take out my phone and take pictures until my hands are so cold, I have to stop and warm them up.

The best thing about the beach is that it's empty. New Jersey is crowded. Most of the time I don't mind, but it's nice to have a break. Here there is not much besides an old tree stump washed up onto the sand and some gulls floating on waves. They look peaceful despite the fact that the water must be icy cold.

I sit on the stump. I like it here. Maybe I'll live here when I grow up. I guess I'd better check it out in the summer first, though. And talk to Lucy.

Then Carlton is standing beside me, his hands in his jacket pockets, looking out at the water.

"So what do you think?" he asks.

I figure he's out here to bring me back, so I brush off my butt and stand up.

"No hurry," Carlson said. "I came out here to give your uncle some privacy. He got a phone call he had to take. He said it was a work call, but I'm pretty sure it was his ex. He's been trying to get back with her, but it's been slow going."

"Mely?"

"I think that was her name. The one who works at the bookstore and writes fantasy novels?"

"I didn't know he was trying to get back together with her." I feel a little hurt. Uncle Gabe's never mentioned it to me.

"He told me in the car while you were asleep." Carlton smooths down his big golden mustache. "Now don't get all jelly. People tend to confide in me. I don't know why. I'm the keeper of the secrets!"

I look at Carlton. I don't know what it is about him, but I can understand that. I trust him too, for some reason. "Were you really my mom's friend?"

"I was her best friend. And she was mine, too, for a long time. Your mom was there for me when no one else was. I miss her."

It feels good to hear someone say that. Nana never says it. Uncle Gabe doesn't either. "I do too sometimes."

I surprise myself when those words come out.

"She'd be glad to know that."

I want to ask him how he can be so sure. Instead I ask, "What was I like when I was little?"

"Oh my God! You were a hellion! You had this huge headful of knotted-up white hair because you would never let anyone comb it, you kicked anyone who crossed you, and your mouth! You cursed like a sailor! Adults were shocked, seriously."

"Yeah, that got me into a lot of trouble when I started school."

"I just bet it did, little girl! But I didn't see as much of you or your mom after I moved down to Philly. And then you went to live with your nana, and I moved out to LA."

"Why did you move out there?"

"My career wasn't going so great on the East Coast." Carlton touches his mustache again. "And I had my own problems to straighten out. I was kind of like your mom. I was hanging out with the wrong people and getting into a bunch of bad habits. I needed a fresh start. So I left. I had to."

"Why didn't Mom do that?" I ask.

"She hadn't figured it out yet. Before she could, those friends got her into a whole pile of trouble she couldn't talk her way out of." For a moment Carlton looks older. "I was lucky. Your mom wasn't so lucky."

He knows about Mom and the drugs, and he knows about Mom and prison, but he doesn't sound mad at her. Or disgusted. I wonder what else he knows about her.

A thin, wavery cry comes from behind us. "Hey!"

Uncle Gabe is standing on the boardwalk, waving his arms like we're miles away. He looks like he doesn't want to step down onto the sand, which makes me smile because it reminds me of a cat that doesn't want to get its paws wet. He cups his hands around his mouth and shouts the words you hear a lot in Jersey. "Let's eat!"

"Guess we better head back," Carlton says to me.

But I have one more question to ask, and it's important. "Carlton—do you have any pictures of me and Mom? Back when I was a kid?"

"Huh. Well, I think I had some on my old phone, and that means they'd be somewhere on one of my laptops, but I'd have to look for them. Don't you have any?" He stops walking when I shake my head. "None?"

I shake my head again.

"You want me to check? I could send them to your uncle Gabe."

"Oh, that would be great!"

"Sure, Franny, I'm glad to help. No promises, okay? But I'll see what I can do."

WHEN WE GET HOME, Nana is in her spot on the sofa. She's basically living there now. Sometimes I really wonder about her. At least she's practicing her Spanish. And our laptop is on the side table, so she was probably chatting with her support group too. "How was the beach?" she asks.

"The beach was great, thanks," my uncle says, taking off his coat. He throws it over the sofa, the way he always does now. I pick it up and take it over to the coat closet. "Did you do your exercises?"

Nana nods. She has physical therapy exercises she's supposed to do every day. She hates them, and for a while she was slacking off, but then some people in her knee injury support group said she needed to keep up with them if she wanted to make a good recovery. She does them religiously now, her face set in a grim line, the way it looks when our toilet overflows.

"What's for dinner?" is her next question.

Uncle Gabe shrugs. "Franny and I aren't hungry."

It's true we had a big, late Italian lunch at this place on the boardwalk, but Nana didn't.

"I'm going to go downstairs and do some work." Uncle Gabe

smiles at me and leaves the room. A moment later I hear the basement door creak open.

I bet you anything he's just going to drink beer out of his mini fridge and watch a movie or play *World of Warcraft*.

"Do you want me to make you something?" I ask Nana. "There are some frozen dinners in the freezer—"

Nana closes her eyes and sighs.

I take a deep breath. I swear, picky eaters are the worst.

"Or I could make you a grilled cheese."

Nana wheels into the kitchen and sets her place for dinner while I make her grilled cheese. There's half a container of takeout tabouleh salad. It's not the best dinner I ever saw, but it could be worse. Nana scooches up to the table to eat. I kind of want to go to my room and look through the pictures I took at the beach, but Nana's been alone all day, so I sit down with her instead. "You want to see my pictures?" I ask. At least that means I'll have a chance to go through them.

For someone who said she didn't want to go to the beach, Nana sure seems interested in my snapshots of driftwood and shadows and gulls on the water. She smiles at the selfies of me and Uncle Gabe goofing around in front of Convention Hall. Then a picture of us with Carlton comes up. Oops, I had forgotten about that one. "Is that—Carlton? Carlton what-was-his-name, his family lived next door—"

"Carlton Ianuzzi," I tell her. "Uncle Gabe asked him to come."

Nana looks as if she's about to say something more, but then changes her mind and goes back to scrolling through the pictures. I watch her and something occurs to me. "Did you want to go with us?"

"Go to a freezing-cold beach and wheel myself up and down the boardwalk for hours?"

I say the obvious: "That's not an answer, Nana."

Nana puts down the phone. She crams a big forkful of tabouleh into her mouth and chews like it requires all of her attention. Which is a trick I know. The "you told me never to talk with my mouth full!" trick. It's a classic. I fold my hands and wait until she's swallowed.

I know she knows I know.

Nana gulps some water to wash down the tabouleh. "Okay, it might have been fun to go. But I wasn't exactly asked."

"Nana! You totally could have come."

"Your uncle asked you. I wasn't mentioned, and I didn't feel like inquiring whether I was included in the invitation. You've probably noticed, but Gabe and I aren't exactly on the best terms. There are reasons for that, none of which concern you, and I don't want you feeling like you need to choose sides. You're having a lot of fun getting to know your uncle, and I don't want to rain on the parade."

Nana puts her utensils in her water glass and her cleared plate in her lap. She pushes away from the table and wheels over to the counter to leave her dishes there.

"But I am getting sick of this house," she says while she has her back to me.

I didn't ask Nana either. I could have said, "Hey, Nana, you come too!" But if she had come, there wouldn't have been room for Carlton in the car. Nana's stuck-out leg takes up the whole back seat. And then I wouldn't have gotten to hear all that stuff about Mom. I mean, that's not fair either, is it?

Especially since Nana will never talk about her.

Nana wheels into the living room and picks up the remote control.

"Do you want to watch something together?" I ask her.

She looks surprised. I guess it has been a while. Uncle Gabe's TV is so much better. "Sure, that would be fun."

"What do you have in mind?" I resign myself to a Carole King concert or *Downton Abbey*.

"I was thinking about *Love It or List It*," Nana says. "What do you think?"

She must mistake my stunned silence for objection, because she says, "A lot of those house-makeover programs are pretty fun to watch. They've been giving me ideas."

"Sure!" I rush to answer, before she changes her mind. I put my phone on the kitchen counter and join her on the couch.

CHAPTER 16

ANOTHER FRIDAY LUNCH, ANOTHER plan for Game Day.

"I have an idea for this weekend," Ruben says. "Something different."

"I think something different would be cool," Arun says. Pretty firmly for Arun, who's always easygoing.

It's been Dungeons & Dragons the last four Sundays. Tate dungeon-mastering every time, crowing whenever he springs one of his nasty surprises on us.

Nana's butt has worn a shiny spot on the upholstery at her favorite end of Mr. Tan's sofa. At least her Spanish has really improved, and the doctor is happy with her knee.

Uncle Gabe spends more and more time in his room watching sports, playing computer games, and drinking beer. It's cool to hang out with my uncle, but I can only deal with so much hockey and *World of Warcraft*. And, to be honest, the way Uncle Gabe creates new characters to run through the same set of instances makes me think of Nana and her TV reruns.

There's something about February. It always drags. I know I would be having more fun if Lucy were here.

"It's a total change of pace." Ruben looks around at us. Me, Arun, Eliot, Tate, and a few other kids from Ruben's chess club. "My sister, Reyna, has a home basketball game tomorrow night, and they've been trying to get good crowds to show up for the games. So instead of doing Dungeons & Dragons on Sunday, maybe we could all go to the game tomorrow night instead. And kind of cheer her on and stuff."

A few people raise their eyebrows. Ruben turns red.

"It was my mom's idea," he adds really quick.

"Is this part of the work-on-Ruben's-social-skills thing?" I say, which makes everyone laugh. Everyone but Ruben.

He shoots me a dirty look that tells me I made the right guess.

Anyway, everyone decides the basketball game is a good idea. A plan to do something different seems to cheer us all up. I think late February can be a good time to try some new things. Lucy used to say that was why she liked to go skiing in the winter. It was something to look forward to so she didn't just stare out the window and think to herself, *Ugh, more snow*.

I just have to figure out how to get to the high school gym tomorrow night.

When lunch is over, I chase after Ruben in the hall.

"Rubes!" He doesn't stop. "Rubes!"

When I finally catch him, he looks at me with his face so blank, I wonder whether he heard me.

"What do you want?" he says.

"Do you think I could get a ride to the game with you?"

"No," Ruben says.

"No?" I wait for him to explain. Maybe he has cousins visiting and the car will be full, or something. But he doesn't add anything more. He just stands there with the totally expressionless face he puts on when he's playing chess.

"Well then, I can't go!" I say.

Ruben shrugs. Then he hitches up his backpack and walks past me into Advanced Math. I'm sure not following him in there.

I CALL LUCY ON my way home from school.

Today I don't wait for her to start complaining about her gingham school uniform (which to be fair sounds completely rancid) or the last mean thing her gran said. Instead I tell her about what happened with Ruben in the hall. "He was being totally unfriendly."

"Well, it's Ruben, right?" Lucy says. "He's often a bit *strange*."

She doesn't get Ruben. To be fair, he doesn't get her, either.

"But, still, I wonder why he would do that," Lucy says.

To give Lucy the full picture, I should mention that talk I had with Ruben about Mom. But given that lately I wonder whether that was a huge mistake, and one of the reasons Ruben is being so weird, I'm going to skip it.

Instead I fill her in on the conversation in the cafeteria. Ruben talking about doing something different. His basketball game plan. And my joke about his social skills.

"Ah," Lucy says.

"I was just kidding around. Do you think I hurt Ruben's feelings?"

"What do *you* think?" For a moment Lucy reminds me of Mr. Burns. Sometimes I think that if Lucy's career as a clay artist doesn't work out, she could be a school counselor.

"Do you think I need to apologize to Ruben?"

"Mum always says an apology can't hurt and a lot of times it helps. She makes us apologize to one another all the time. Apologizing to Ned is *the worst*."

Ugh. It's definitely something to add to the day's list of Things Currently Worrying Franny Petroski.

It's not fair. Ruben never apologizes to me. For some of the clueless junk he says. For being an embarrassing friend sometimes at school. Do I complain? No! And he never says thank you, either.

"Hey, are you still there? You're not mad, are you?" Lucy asks.

I think that over. "I'm not mad at *you*," I say finally.

Lucy laughs. "Franny! I *miss* you."

WHEN I GET HOME, Nana is on the sofa as usual.

"I have something for you." I reach into my backpack and pull out a big slick stack of architecture magazines. I found them in the paper recyclables bin at Studio Club. Miss Midori said it was fine for me to take them home.

"One person's trash, another person's treasure," Miss Midori said. "Like I need to tell you that, Franny."

Nana shuts her laptop and reaches out for the magazines. She's gotten into home design since she started watching HGTV.

"Honeybee! So thoughtful." Nana pinches my cheek. "Grazie!"

"Ow, Nana! Quit." I'm just glad no one else saw.

"How was school? And Studio Club?" Nana asks her usual questions as I go into the kitchen to find the Triscuits.

We've started hiding them from Uncle Gabe. He'll eat them all and he never puts them on the shopping list, which is against the house rules. I hate to admit this, but Uncle Gabe does a lot of things that go against the way Nana and I keep house. He never hangs his coat up or puts anything away after he's done with it. He tracks crap everywhere because he doesn't take off his shoes at the door, and he finishes the best snacks and just waits for us to find out. That's probably the most annoying thing he does. Although hanging up Uncle Gabe's coat has gotten old too.

Nana says her house rules are just common-sense things that make life easier for everyone. If she's feeling tired or cranky, she'll also add that she's not the maid. I'm not always the biggest fan of stuff Nana says, but she's *totally* in the right on this one.

"School was okay," I say. "What did you do today?"

159

"Grace brought lunch over. I chatted with my knee injury group, I did my exercises and Spanish." I can feel Nana studying me while I put a plate of crackers by her. "Are you worried about something?"

"Why would I be worried?" Ugh! Why do I have to have the kind of face that gives everything away?

"I don't know. You tell me."

I don't want to get into the whole Ruben thing with Nana. "Ruben wants a bunch of us to go to the basketball game tomorrow night at the high school. Because Reyna is playing? But, um, he can't give me a ride."

Nana does not pick up on the highly suspect fact that Ruben is not giving me a ride. "The game's in the high school gymnasium?"

"Uh-huh. Maybe Uncle Gabe could give me a ride. Or you could call me an Uber," I suggest.

"A twelve-year-old girl on her own in an Uber? I don't think so. But we'll get you to that game one way or another. Don't worry about that."

UNCLE GABE IS NOT taking me to the basketball game. He's having Zoom drinks tonight with his friends in Madison.

Nana and Aunt Gravy are taking me. And that's because they're going too!

This is not what I had in mind.

"Are you sure there's a door your wheelchair will fit through?" I ask Nana while we're waiting for Aunt Gravy, who's late as usual.

"There won't be a problem. I called Adela and asked about the handicapped access. Of course she knew—Adela knows everything. There's a handicapped entrance with a ramp, and seating right on the floor. The only problem might be the bathrooms. I need to make sure I don't drink too much soda."

"What if someone bumps into your leg or something?"

"Franny, the people in my support group are doing all kinds of things with their legs in full extension. It doesn't stop them. One of them—this guy in Texas—danced with his daughter at her wedding last week! He posted some great pictures. If they can do it, I can do it too."

How do you tell your nana you'd rather she just dropped you off?

"Don't worry," Nana says with her mind-reading skills in full operation. "You can sit with your friends. Gracie and I won't be embarrassing. We'll act like we don't know you."

JUST BEFORE GAME TIME, we pull into one of the handicapped parking spaces outside the gym. Before Aunt Gravy has turned off the engine, Nana gets out a ten-dollar bill and hands it to me. "That's enough for a ticket and a snack. Meet us here at the car after the game is over. And text me if you're running late."

"Do you need me to help you get out?" I ask.

"We've got it," Aunt Gravy says.

"Go find your friends," Nana says.

I keep on sitting. "What's going on?" Nana asks. "Are we forgetting something?"

They haven't forgotten anything. It's just that I don't know how Ruben is going to act when I show up. I'm pretty sure he doesn't want me here.

Aunt Gravy and Nana look at each other. Aunt Gravy says, "Tell you what. We'll save you a seat by us, and if you want to bounce back and forth between us and your friends, you can. That's what my nieces and nephews used to do."

"Fine," Nana says.

That works for me, too.

Maybe Aunt Gravy isn't so bad.

I think I'm going to try calling her Aunt Gracie. She can be really nice sometimes. And I've noticed lately she doesn't smell nearly as much like gravy anymore.

Inside, the gym is already pretty full. I'm looking around when I hear someone shout "Franny!" I think it was Eliot. I spot a familiar bunch of people sitting far up in the bleachers. There's our Game Day crowd, of course, but there are also some people from the Chess Club and the Asian American Club and a few other people I don't know. Ruben has more friends than I thought.

Arun catches my eye and grins as I sit down next to him. Eliot leans forward and waves. Tate gives me a smirk, like he's surprised I'm here.

Ruben, he doesn't even turn his head.

He's telling Arun about some new fish his mom got for their aquarium. A lionfish.

Arun says, "Cool! No way would my mom let me get one of those. They die too easily."

"My mom's a total fish whisperer, she can handle it. And we think they're just generally cool. I mean, they're poisonous—"

What?! Seriously?

Why would someone have a poisonous fish in their aquarium? I say in my head.

Only it's another one of those times when I don't manage to keep my words inside.

Ruben finally takes notice of me. His look is definitely not friendly as he says, "What's the big deal? If you know what you're doing, they're not going to hurt you." He rolls his eyes the way Tate likes to do.

"Uh, sometimes they hurt people," Arun says.

"No, they actually don't," Ruben says.

Arun doesn't back down the way a lot of people do when Ruben corrects them. "I've heard sometimes they do. That you have to be careful. And they'll eat your other fish."

"Ours doesn't," Ruben says. "It wasn't eating much of anything for a while, but Mom finally got it eating fresh shrimp. She's working on frozen squid now."

He's back to talking to Arun like I'm not there. I feel invisible. I listen to them chat about fish until the music starts up and the basketball players run onto the court. Nana and Aunt Gracie are down courtside. They actually have excellent seats. They're eating popcorn and it looks like Nana is breaking her rule about drinking soda.

It feels like everyone around me is talking and laughing and having a good time. I wish I could do that too, but Ruben's back turned to me ruins everything.

I decide to ignore him, too, but the lonely feeling gets worse and worse until finally I feel my eyes fill up with tears.

Oh great!

To burst into tears during a basketball game—that will convince everyone I'm the coolest kid in sixth grade.

I jump up and head to the girls' bathroom. It's this gross, sweaty little box crammed in by the locker rooms, but at least it's empty. I sit down on the toilet in one of the stalls.

So stupid Ruben Yao doesn't like me anymore. Fine! So what? I don't need him.

Lucy swears by crying. "Just go ahead and do it" is Lucy's motto. She says crying always makes her feel better, but it doesn't work the same way for me.

I mean, crying doesn't change anything. I found that out when I was a lot littler than I am now.

Plus, when I do it, my face gets all pink and puffy.

I wash my face with cold water and press wet paper towels to my eyes. I peer at myself in the mirror. I'm pretty sure I look all right, so I head back out to the bleachers.

When I get back, the halftime show is on.

Arun leans over and whispers, "Are you okay?"

I whisper back, "Yes. How come?"

"Your eyes are kind of pink."

I cast around for an excuse. "I have allergies," I tell him.

When the halftime show ends, there's a break before the game starts back up. A line forms at the concession stand, and a buzz of talk breaks out again all around me. Ruben and Tate are laughing hard about something. They lift their hands and slap them together.

When Tate first started hanging out with us, I thought it wouldn't last long. That Ruben would figure out how annoying Tate is—how he has to run everything, have the last word in every argument, and win every game.

But . . . you know what? I'm not sure that's going to happen.

I'll bet you anything the spare seat in Dr. Yao's car was occupied by Tate's butt.

I say to Arun, "I think I'm going to go down and sit with my nana for a while."

"Oh, okay," Arun says. Then he adds, talking fast, "Hey, I've been thinking. We could get together and play card games or whatever when we feel like it. You and me and Eliot. And anyone else who's interested."

He says this like it's no big deal, but I notice he's keeping his voice kind of low. I think that's so Ruben won't hear.

"Not at Ruben's?" I know I probably sound thick, but I want to make sure I understand.

"Well, it's just that Ruben never wants to play stuff like Munchkin, you know? And when we're at his house, we have to play what he wants."

"But we'd *invite* Ruben." I make sure that's clear.

"Of course," Arun says.

Because even if Ruben didn't want to play Yahtzee or Gyrating Hamsters or whatever, he would be super hurt if we didn't invite him.

"That sounds like fun. We could probably play at my house sometimes if we want, but I'd need to ask my nana first."

"Cool. Eliot's all for it too."

Ruben and Tate burst out laughing again.

I tell Arun goodbye. He's the only one who seems to notice as I step down the bleachers toward Nana and Aunt Gracie. It takes a while to get there because it seems like everyone else has come up with the same plan and is also switching seats. It's like a game of musical chairs in the gym. By the time I get down to the handicapped seats, the whistle blows and the slapping feet and grunts of the basketball game are in full swing again.

And Nana is nowhere in sight. It's just Aunt Gracie sitting by herself surrounded by two empty seats.

Oh great.

CHAPTER 17

I GET A LITTLE NERVOUS talking to Aunt Gracie. We don't have much to talk about, so she ends up asking me a million dumb adult questions about my favorite classes and junk like that. But one glance back toward Ruben and Tate and I plop my butt right down next to her. "Hi, Aunt Gracie. Where's Nana?" I ask.

"She went to get a snack a while ago. I think she's still over there."

I look at the concession stand. Sure enough, Nana is at one side in her wheelchair. She has another bag of popcorn in her hand, but she's not eating it. She's staring at the basketball game, and I get the feeling she's not really watching that. She looks deep in thought about something else.

"Your nana is annoyed with me, I'm afraid," Aunt Gracie says.

Annoyed at Aunt Gracie? She might be embarrassing to be seen with, and kind of awkward, but she works so hard to be inoffensive, it's hard to imagine how someone could be annoyed with her. Especially Nana. Nana loves her. "What happened?" I ask before I can stop and think.

"I offered an opinion she took issue with. She told me I didn't know what I was talking about, which wasn't true. I reminded her of that fact, and then she took herself off to the refreshment stand and there she is now."

A ball bounces in our direction, and Reyna swoops in and scoops it up before it can go out of bounds. I'm pretty sure we get a few drops of her sweat on us.

Do adults do this kind of stuff too—get mad over little things and stop talking to each other?

Ugh! That's discouraging. I was hoping that when I got out of middle school, it wouldn't be a problem anymore. Does it never get better?

"An opinion about what?" I ask Aunt Gracie.

Aunt Gracie looks even more embarrassed than she usually does. "Something that your nana wants to keep to herself right now."

A lightbulb comes on in my brain. They were probably talking about me! I mean, what else could it have been?

"Were you talking about me?" I hear myself ask. "Aunt Gravy, come on. Please tell me."

"What did you just call me?" Aunt Gracie says.

Oh crap.

"Did you say 'Aunt Gravy'?"

"Um—no."

If you can't think of anything else to say, try lying! Only usually it doesn't work all that well. Like right now. Aunt Gracie looks so hurt, I feel worse than before. Maybe I should just go back to the girls' bathroom.

Thank God, Nana is coming toward us. The people on the sidelines move out of her way. I don't know what Aunt Gravy said to her, but it's true Nana doesn't look happy. She looks more like the way she used to: grumpy and tired.

Hey, that's a weird thought.

Just a few months back, Nana went to work and came home and pretty much the rest of her free time was spent in front of our TV. She didn't do much of anything and she almost never wanted to go anywhere, even though she wasn't in a wheelchair then and she could have gone wherever she wanted.

Now Nana's in a wheelchair, but it's like her world has gotten bigger instead of smaller. She's learning Spanish. She's on her laptop with the people in her support group. She's watching new TV shows. And she's coming to basketball games, wheelchair and all.

When did all that happen? How did that happen?

"Gracie, my leg hurts," Nana says. "Do you think we could head home?" I'm pretty sure Nana is lying about her leg hurting. She hasn't been complaining about that for a while. "Franny, maybe you can catch a ride with Ruben. What are you doing here anyway? I thought you wanted to hang out with your friends."

"I think she was checking up on you," Aunt Gracie says.

I wait to see whether she mentions the "Aunt Gravy" incident. She doesn't, but I notice she's not really looking at me either.

She's acting like Ruben.

I'm a terrible person.

"I think maybe I'll just come home too if that's all right," I say.

"Did anything happen?" Nana's gaze lingers on my face. In another moment, I think she's going to mention that it's pinker than usual.

"My allergies are bothering me," I say real quick.

THE RIDE HOME IS almost silent. It's weird because Nana and Aunt Gracie usually chat nonstop. When my phone buzzes, it sounds extra loud. I dig it out of my pocket.

Hey, where are you? We're going to get ice cream at Sonny's. A second later it goes again: *This is Arun, by the way. Eliot's mom said you can ride with us if you want.*

Great.

I could have gone for ice cream with my friends instead of sitting all by myself in the back of a cold car that still smells like gravy, even if Aunt Gracie doesn't.

At our house, Aunt Gracie just drops us off instead of coming in. She always comes in, even just for a second, but not tonight. She waits to make sure Nana gets up the ramp okay, and then her headlights swing out of our driveway and vanish up the street.

Inside, Uncle Gabe is stretched out on the sofa. The TV isn't on. The radio isn't on. Mr. Tan's stereo, either. Just Uncle Gabe staring up at the ceiling.

"How was your Zoom party?" Nana asks. She leans forward in her wheelchair so she can take off her coat and then wheels over to the closet to hang it up. Halfway there she has to stop. Uncle Gabe has left his shoes in the middle of the floor again. I go over and pick them up.

He frowns at the ceiling. "Don and Mely were being all kissy-kissy tonight. Kind of weird and annoying. Like being back in high school and seeing all those couples making out in the hallways."

Yeech. I'm so not ready for high school.

Nana says, "I thought you said they'd been dating for a while."

"But nothing all that serious." Uncle Gabe shoots her an annoyed look. "Tonight she was sitting on his *lap*."

"Sounds like it's serious now." Nana sighs. "I'm sorry."

Uncle Gabe sits up and rubs his face. "And, on that happy note, I'm going downstairs."

The basement door closes hard behind him. That means he doesn't want company while he watches *Die Hard* or *Lethal Weapon* or whatever movie he picks tonight.

Nana wheels over to the side table, picks up the water glass Uncle Gabe left there, and brings it over to the sink. Nana's clearing away his dishes, I'm moving his shoes. My uncle needs to learn how to clean up after himself. "Do you want the bathroom first, or can I go?" she asks me.

"Are you going to bed already? It's barely nine o'clock."

"Well, I'm tired," Nana says.

She looks tired.

After she's in bed, I sit out in the living room by myself, the same way Uncle Gabe did.

Uncle Gabe downstairs in his room, alone.

Nana in her room, alone.

Me out here, alone.

We are the biggest bunch of losers on the planet.

There's only one thing I can think of to make anything better. But it does mean I have to break one of Nana's rules. I turn on my phone and call Ruben.

"Hello?" he shouts into the phone.

I can hear all kinds of voices surrounding him on his end.

"Ruben?" I can't shout. If I do, Nana will hear me and remind me my phone is supposed to be off by now. "Listen, I'm sorry about what I said yesterday. That dumb joke I made."

The ruckus on Ruben's end dies down. I think maybe he went outside. "*Which* dumb joke?" Ruben says, like I tell stupid jokes all the time.

"About your social skills. I'm sorry."

"Look, I can't talk. I'm here at Sonny's with everybody and

Mom is tapping her watch. I'm not supposed to be on my phone after nine."

"Me neither," I remind him.

He hangs up without saying that he wishes I were at Sonny's too, or that I should make sure I come next time.

"Franny?" Nana's voice floats down the hall. "Can you come in here?"

Oh great.

I walk as slowly as I can down to Nana's bedroom. Nana is sitting up against her pillows, rubbing lotion into her hands. Her wheelchair is by the bed, ready for her to get into it in the morning. "Who were you talking to? I heard you say you were sorry."

I shrug. I know better than to be rude to Nana, but why can't she just leave me alone right now?

"Who are you apologizing to? You're not supposed to be on your phone this time of night."

"No one, okay?"

"No one? Some stranger you met on the Internet?"

"Nana! We had the stranger danger talk at school *last year*."

"Listen, young lady, I don't know where this attitude of yours is coming from. And just when I caught you being nice to your aunt Gracie for a change, too. Maybe you're practicing being a teenager, I have no idea, but it's not going to fly around here."

Ugh!

"Whatever," I hear myself say.

Nana snaps her fingers. "Phone. Now."

I go forward as slowly as I can and hand Nana my phone. I give it one last longing look as she turns it off and puts it into her nightstand drawer.

"Now go to bed," she says.

I linger a moment. "When can I have my phone back?"

"When I decide you can have it back. And the more times you ask, the longer I keep it. Go to bed, Frances! I am *not* in the mood."

CHAPTER 18

SUNDAY DRAGS.

Nana is out in the living room on her laptop. I can hear the keys clattering and it makes me wonder if there's some crisis in the knee injury group. But I'm not asking. I'm not talking to Nana right now, not any more than I have to. And I don't care about a bunch of old people arguing over whether gluten-free diets can help them heal faster.

Uncle Gabe is downstairs "working."

Really, he's playing *World of Warcraft*. He has his mic on and I can hear him talking about hit points and where they can find a healer for some instance they want to run.

When he first came here, and we did some fun stuff, I thought that might keep on happening. But he's getting as bad as Nana about just hanging out at home. Maybe worse.

My phone is nowhere in sight, and I know better than to ask about it.

Ugh!

I guess at least I can get some laundry done.

I drag Nana's hamper downstairs.

I put her clothes in and then I'm actually so bored, I start wandering around the basement, looking at all the things stacked up and leaning against the walls.

The duffel bag of Mom's clothes is still down here. I want to sneak it upstairs, but with Nana here all the time, it's not easy. And that black plastic kite is propped up against the shelves. I still have no idea what to do with it.

I wander by two pieces of an old broken ladder, some empty picture frames, a plastic bag crammed full of other plastic bags, a laundry basket half full of Christmas ribbon, some old pieces of plywood. There are bags of old clothes. A cookie tin that jingles when I shake it, and when I open it it's full of sewing things. Scissors, buttons, pins, measuring tape, iron-on patches . . .

There's lots of interesting junk down here now that I've stopped and looked. You know. Basement objects.

My art brain starts to stir around.

Even if it is kind of slow and creaky, like Nana waking up after a too-long nap.

People put stuff like this away, like it can never matter again, or make any difference.

But I think (and Miss Midori does too) that sometimes things like this are only waiting to be noticed. Waiting to be given another chance, their new purpose.

Maybe the people who hide these remnants in their attics

and basements know that. They must in some way. Otherwise, why wouldn't Mr. Tan have just shoved all this "junk" into the garbage?

I pick up one of the picture frames. Both the glass and the back are gone, and it's super dusty. It's a cheapie, the kind of frame you pick up at the drugstore for a few bucks.

It makes me think of the tabletop looms we used when we did a weaving unit in art in elementary school. Frame looms, the teacher called them. They were mega basic. But sometimes those basic things can be the best. We tied our pieces of yarn at the top and bottom of the frame to form a warp, and then we wove our other materials in and out across. Most of us used yarn from a big bin. But I remember the teacher saying that you could use all kinds of different things for weaving. Anything long, skinny, and flexible.

Wire, plastic, ribbon, torn-up cloth. They all can work.

I drag one of those bags of clothes into the middle of the basement floor and tear it open.

And then I haul over some of the things from the shelves— the cookie tin, the Christmas ribbon, and the plastic bags.

I sit down on the floor and put the picture frame on my lap. I dust it with my sleeve and then I start tying long pieces of Christmas ribbon to the top and bottom of the frame, making a warp. When I'm done with that, I pull some clothes out of the bag and start cutting them into strips.

It seems like it's just a few minutes later when Uncle Gabe says, "Franny, it's dinnertime."

I blink, looking at him. Then I put the frame down and stand up and stretch. I rub my back, the way Nana does after a long day of work.

My butt is cold from sitting on the floor, my back hurts, and I can see through one of Uncle Gabe's bedroom windows that it's dark outside. But I'm happy.

It's one of the best things about art: how it can make time just melt away and turn a long, boring day into a good day.

Miss Midori says, "When you make art, ideas become things." And it always feels great to make an idea into a thing.

Dinner is quiet until Uncle Gabe says, "Franny was working on something cool down there in the basement."

Nana blinks. "Really. What?"

I just shrug. I don't like to talk about my projects while I'm working on them.

Uncle Gabe says, "She was weaving something, using a picture frame. With rags and plastic bags and wire. It was looking great! All bumpy, with lots of different colors—"

"Where did you get a picture frame?" Nana asks me.

Uh-oh. I know where Nana is going with this. "It was in the basement."

Nana puts down her fork.

"Nana, it didn't have glass or a back. It looked like it was junk that someone hadn't thrown out yet."

"But maybe Mr. Tan was saving it for something. You don't know. Maybe *he* likes to do art projects with old picture frames. We're renting this house. We don't own it or the things he left in it. You can't just assume that anything you come across is okay to commandeer because you want it for one of your art projects."

She practically puts quotes with her fingers around "art projects."

To Nana, "art" is a picture that someone does with pencils or paint and then puts in a frame. I'm pretty sure she thinks a lot of my stuff doesn't qualify.

I stab at my eggplant parmigiana.

"Ma, it was definitely junk," Uncle Gabe confirms. "And so were those old bags of clothes."

"Bags of clothes!" Nana says. "Frances, how do you know those weren't Mr. Tan's out-of-season clothes?"

I think of the pair of burgundy sweatpants I cut up. They had holes in both knees and the waist elastic was gone. People around here throw away totally fine clothes, without any holes at all, so I think I was safe. But it's true I didn't ask Mr. Tan. Maybe I should have. Maybe I messed up.

Again.

Uncle Gabe mutters something. Then he says, "After dinner I'll call Dr. Yao and ask about the stuff in the basement."

"There's no need to bother the Yaos," Nana starts.

"No, no!" My uncle holds up his fork. "I insist."

Nana doesn't look at me as she says, "You have pads of art paper and a whole box full of supplies. Crayons. Colored pencils. Paints. Why don't you ever use any of that?"

I do use them, just not all the time. But what's the point of saying any of this to Nana? It's not like she *wants* to understand!

After we've finished dinner and the dishes, I go back downstairs and look at my picture frame project. This time, it seems lumpy and dumb. The cheap frame. All the knots in the fabric where I tied different pieces together. Like something a kindergartener would make.

It probably *is* just a bunch of junk, the way Nana would describe it.

I should go out and ditch it in the trash.

"Calm down, Frances." I'm all alone, so I say it out loud.

Before I throw it away, I'll show it to Miss Midori.

"Always save your drafts," she says to us. Miss Midori isn't just a visual artist, she also writes poems. What she means is: always show someone else what you did before you decide it's terrible.

I wish Lucy were here. She always looks at my projects, the same way I'll always look at hers if she asks.

Maybe it's not so terrible. Uncle Gabe said he liked it.

Then I hear Uncle Gabe coming downstairs.

"Okay, I just talked to Ruben's mom. She said that anything down here that looks like junk is junk. You're welcome to use it however you want. She said Mr. Tan's barely been down here for years."

That's good to know. "Did you tell Nana?"

"I did," my uncle says. "I don't think she'll hassle you about it again."

He squeezes my shoulder. He's not the touchiest person. I think he probably could tell how upset I was at dinner.

"Uncle Gabe, why doesn't Nana like the things I make?"

Uncle Gabe sticks his hand into his hair, the same way Nana always does. "Let's not be dramatic. She likes a lot of your art. She signed you up for Studio Club, remember, and that materials fee wasn't cheap. But some of this stuff you do, I think it reminds her of your mom. Mia was always coming home with treasures she'd found on the street or gotten out of dumpsters. She'd use a hubcap for a fruit bowl or a file cabinet to store her clothes. She loved repurposing things, like you do. And any way you resemble your mom is going to worry your nana. I'm sorry, Franny, but that's just the way it is."

I look down at my weaving. I'd never thought about how

my dumpster diving and garbage recycling might have come from Mom.

I think it's cool she did that.

I think anyone who thought like that can't be all bad. No matter what people say, or won't say, about her.

"Reduce, reuse, recycle," I say.

Uncle Gabe slaps his thigh. "That's exactly what Mia used to say! Where did you learn that?"

I don't remember. I mean, where did I "learn" to be a vegetarian? Mom must have taught me that, too, but I don't remember anything about it. When it comes to Mom, so many things are fuzzy.

THE NEXT DAY I get to school early and take my weaving to the art room to show Miss Midori.

She says, "Oh, I *like* that. All those different textures. And those big knots, they make it. They're begging to be touched, aren't they?"

And just like that, I go from thinking my weaving is garbage-can worthy to thinking maybe it's okay.

"Do you think it's done?" Miss Midori asks. I've noticed this is her way of implying it's not.

There are a few minutes left before school starts, so I sit down to look at it again. I don't want to rush. That's not the way my brain works. Especially not the art-brain part. Outside, the hallways are getting noisier. I suddenly hear Tate's voice cutting through the buzz, saying, "Oh, *right*." The way he likes to say it. Mega sarcastically. Ruben is probably with him.

I'm out of time. I put my weaving in my cubby and wash my hands: I got glitter on them from somewhere in here. "The devil's sparkles"—that's what Miss Midori calls glitter. I get a whiff of wet paper towel, and all of a sudden I'm back in kindergarten.

In those days Ruben washed his hands a lot. He hated for them to be dirty. He also wouldn't wear socks and he always carried around this stuffed dolphin in his backpack. The dolphin is still on top of his dresser in his room. It's called Lumba-Lumba. Ruben was what Nana called "slightly eccentric." Some of the other boys liked to pick on him, and one day Aiden Houston grabbed Lumba-Lumba and wouldn't give it back, and Ruben started to cry.

I went over to Aiden and took the dolphin away, and when Aiden tried to grab Lumba-Lumba back, I shoved him so hard that he fell down. Then I kicked him, right in the butt. He was the one crying then, the big baby. I got sent home from kindergarten for two days and Aiden's mom tried to argue that I belonged in a special classroom because I had "anger issues" and was "out of control," and she and Nana had a huge fight about it.

I barely remember any of this, but I know all the deets because both Nana and Dr. Yao love to tell this story.

Anyway, as weird as it might sound, that was when Dr. Yao called Nana and asked whether we'd like to have a playdate sometime. That was when Ruben and I really became friends.

I guess whatever happens with Ruben and me, we'll always have kindergarten.

CHAPTER 19

HOW WAS SCHOOL, HONEYBEE?" Nana asks from her perch on the couch.

I drop my wet coat over a chair and then catch a look from Nana and hang it up. Uncle Gabe's habits are wearing off on me.

"Not great, huh?" Nana knows me too well.

A bunch of Tate's friends sat with us at lunch today. I swear they spent the whole time talking about D&D characters. Ruben glanced my way a few times, but I noticed he didn't offer me any of his pancit. I guess he's still stewing, but I don't think apologizing again is going to make a difference.

"Lunch was pretty dire," is all I say. "Ruben has some boring new friends."

"You two will work it out." Nana closes her laptop. "Just as long as there wasn't any biting or kicking involved."

"Nana, I'm not in kindergarten anymore!"

I get an apple from the bowl on the counter. Then I pick up another one, hold it up, and look at Nana. She nods, and I lob it over. She catches it perfectly and polishes it on her sleeve.

That's something Nana always does with apples, and it makes me feel a little better, like even when everything is shifting and quaking, there's still some solid ground.

"I didn't have the greatest day either," Nana says. "I had to apologize to Gracie, and I hate apologizing."

I try to look uninterested. "What did you do to Aunt Gracie?"

"I asked for her advice about something, and she offered me an opinion that I didn't want to hear. I got mad and then I was rude." Nana shrugs. "It was more my fault because I had *asked* for her opinion. But one thing about Gracie—she never holds a grudge."

I hope so, I think, remembering my Aunt Gravy remark. I bite into the apple. I'm always hungry after school.

"Apologizing is something your mom was never good at," Nana says out of nowhere. "She just hated doing it. Sometimes it seemed like she'd do anything to avoid saying 'I'm sorry.' Along with 'I was wrong.'" Nana polishes her apple again. "Maybe she got that from me. What? What's with the face?"

"Could you tell me something good about Mom?"

"Something good?"

"Something about her that was good. Besides hating to apologize and breaking the law and having to go to jail and not taking care of me and all that." I almost say the words "bipolar disorder," but I don't have quite enough courage. "There must have been some good things about her."

Nana opens and shuts her mouth. Finally she says, "There were a lot of good things about your mom."

"Okay, so let's hear them," I say.

Nana puts her laptop on the side table and gives me her full attention. "She was a gifted artist and singer. She had a lot of charisma. All she had to do was walk out on a stage to command everyone's attention. She hated bullies, and she'd stand up to them, every time. That's part of the reason she and Carlton were so close. Carlton had such a hard time for a while! His own dad was on him not to be so girly, and he got bullied relentlessly at school. Your mom stood up for him. *Every single time*. She didn't care who she was telling off! Popular kids, teachers, the principal—Mia would say what was on her mind. Those were times I was so proud of her."

Nana starts to laugh. And then, just to surprise me, she wipes her eyes. I'm not sure whether I should go over and hug her or not. But before I can move, she says, "Now, your turn. Your turn to say something good about your mom."

I open my mouth to say what I usually do, that I was too little to have any memories, but then I stop and think. "Well, she had good taste in music. Her lap was really comfortable. I think she rocked me to sleep a lot. And when we were in the car, I remember she didn't make me stay in my car seat unless I wanted to."

Nana clears her throat. "Yes. I remember getting you out of that habit."

She waits to see if I say anything else. When I don't, Nana reaches over for her laptop and takes a bite from her apple.

I wander downstairs to find Uncle Gabe. Maybe he has time for a quick walk or chat. And I've been thinking about those pictures Carlton said he would look for. Maybe Uncle Gabe heard from him and forgot to tell me.

Uncle Gabe's door is closed, like he's working. But I don't hear him talking on the phone. And I don't hear any loud punk music, the kind he likes to listen to while he's programming.

I knock. "Uncle Gabe? Can I come in?"

"Okay."

Uncle Gabe is lying on his bed staring up at the ceiling.

"Are you feeling all right?"

My uncle sighs. "Mely is marrying Don Hollenbeck."

"That's—"

I'm about to say "nice," because that's what you're supposed to say, but the look on my uncle's face lets me know that would be the wrong word.

"Awful," I finish.

"I *introduced* them! They've been dating maybe six months! Don told me they weren't all that serious—and now they're engaged! I had to act happy for them when Don told me. And not only am I invited to the wedding, Don wants me to be an usher! So I have to figure out a way to get out of *that*!" My uncle grabs one of his pillows and puts it over his head.

This is so obviously not the time to ask my uncle about Carlton's pictures. I edge out backward and close the door.

"How was work today, Gabe?" Nana asks at dinner.

We're having Thai delivery. I'm not surprised. Today doesn't seem like one of the times when Uncle Gabe whips up a feast. He's a good cook, but he has to be in the right mood.

"Not the best. Wall-to-wall meetings," my uncle says, sounding cranky.

That isn't true, unless you count lying on his bed with a pillow over his head being in a meeting.

"Honeybee, I had a good idea," Nana says. "I was thinking about how disappointed you were about the French Club trip, and then I remembered something. Eastern Canada is French-speaking!"

I vaguely remember hearing that somewhere, but I'm not sure what it has to do with the French Club trip.

"So let's go to Montreal this summer," Nana continues. "You can practice your French there. We'll ask Aunt Gracie to come with us. I get nervous traveling on my own, but with another adult it's fine."

I'm not sure what I'm most surprised about.

That Nana is suggesting we take a trip?

That Nana is admitting traveling makes her nervous?

Or that I might actually be going somewhere? Somewhere that isn't here?

Other people's families do fun "weekend breaks," as Dr. Yao calls them. The same way other people's families have parties. Is this really my life? Or have I slipped into some parallel world, the way it happened in *Sal and Gabi Break the Universe*? In this universe, Nana is fun-loving and energetic and not . . . well, scared of everything. I like this universe, but I'm not sure it's mine.

"How are you planning to get there? You know it's like a seven-hour drive from here, right? And that's on the *highway*." Uncle Gabe says this in a way that reminds me of Tate: like he's trying to bring everyone around him down. We all know Nana is scared of driving on the highway.

Nana smiles. I think she was waiting for Uncle Gabe to bring this up. "We'll take the train. Amtrak runs to Montreal. It's called the Adirondack train."

Uncle Gabe looks annoyed. "That probably takes forever, Ma."

"It does," Nana says. "Ten hours. But what do we care? It's a beautiful ride along the Hudson River and through upstate New York. Franny can bring her sketch pad."

"That sounds awesome!"

"You're welcome to join us, Gabe," Nana says.

"Oh, I'll be back in Madison by then." He pushes down the lid of his takeout container over his uneaten pad thai. That means he's done eating, and in another moment he'll disappear downstairs. I need to grab my chance.

"Hey, Uncle Gabe! Have you heard from Carlton since we went to the beach? He was going to look for some old pictures to send me."

"Franny," my uncle says. In that one word, he reproaches me for bringing up something as trivial as pictures while he has a broken heart. "No. I haven't."

"Pictures? What pictures?" Nana says, sounding more like her old suspicious self. I'm sure she's thinking about stranger danger again.

"Just some pictures of me and Mom when I was little. Carlton said he would look for them. Only, I haven't heard anything. I thought maybe Uncle Gabe could ask him."

"Carlton Ianuzzi?" Nana asks. I wait for her to say that she's never liked that Carlton person, but instead she says, "Could you ask him, Gabe? I'm sure Franny would love some pictures. She has barely any pictures of her and Mia together."

"Why would she want them?" my uncle snaps. "Why would she want to remember any of that?"

"She's curious about her mother," Nana says. "It's totally normal."

Since when does Nana say anything like that about my Mom questions? Whatever happened to "I'm too tired"?

"Look, I barely know the guy! He was Mia's friend, not mine. And I've had just about enough of Mia for one trip east. I've reached my limit. I don't want to talk about Mia! I don't want to look at pictures of her! I don't want to find her! If I saw her on the street, I would turn around and walk in the other direction and hope she didn't see me!"

There's this roaring in my ears. Like what Uncle Gabe just said has filled them up and there's no room for anything else.

"Fine," Nana says.

"It was bad enough growing up—"

"Gabriel, you made your point." Nana helps herself to another spoonful of pad thai.

"Fine." My uncle sounds like Nana at her grumpiest.

She says, "On another note, do you two remember what's happening tomorrow?"

Happening?

Uncle Gabe looks up at the ceiling. "I'm hoping it's not someone's birthday."

Ugh. He's the worst! Doesn't he know when our birthdays are?

But why would he? It's not like he ever sent a card or a present.

Nana clears her throat. "Just a reminder, I'm in September and your niece is in July. No, what's happening is that I'm going to see my orthopedist. If I'm lucky, I'll finally be getting my leg out of extension."

Nana's only been in the wheelchair for two months, but it seems like forever.

"What happens then?" I ask her.

"I'll get a walker and a knee brace, and I'll start physical therapy." Nana smiles. "At last! Pretty soon I'll be cooking dinner and getting back behind the wheel—everything I used to do."

"That's good news," Uncle Gabe says. "And good timing."

Nana and I both stop eating to look at my uncle. Nana literally has her fork halfway to her mouth. It's like when you stop a movie to hop off the sofa and go get a snack.

Ruben and I used to love to see the freeze-frames when we did that. I wonder if he and Tate do it now.

"Because I was thinking it's about time for me to head back to Madison," my uncle says. "I was looking at flights this afternoon and there are some good prices right now."

"I don't understand," my grandmother says. "What's the hurry?"

"Hurry? I've been here almost two months!"

Nana nods. "More like six weeks. And Franny and I really appreciate everything you've done, but I was hoping you could stick around a few weeks longer."

I can see Uncle Gabe swallow. "Ma, I have to go talk to

Mely. She can't marry Don. There's got to be a way to change her mind."

"Gabe, that is a terrible idea."

"Ma!"

Nana doesn't look mean, though. Just sad. "You're going to make a fool out of yourself and you're not going to change her mind. I'm sorry to have to tell you that, but it's true. Can't you give us a little more time? Pretty soon I'll be able to start putting some weight on my leg. Everyone in the knee injury group says that things start getting a whole lot easier then."

Uncle Gabe just shakes his head.

Something's bubbling away inside me now. Slowly. It's like the polenta Aunt Gracie made for us once. She let me stand by the stove on a chair and watch. She said I couldn't be too close because it was dangerous, and once the polenta was almost done, I could see what she meant. When it gets thick, these big bubbles start coming up. They kind of bulge up out of it and then burst. And when they burst, watch out! Hot polenta spatters *everywhere* and will give you the nastiest burns!

I can feel the bubbles coming up inside me—slow, thick, and super hot.

I take a deep breath. I take another one.

"Franny, do you have an opinion?" Nana asks. "About what Uncle Gabe should do?"

I try counting to ten and give up at three. Uncle Gabe is

watching me, and I make sure I'm looking back at him when I say, "If he wants to go, he should go. Whatever."

I get to my room without what Nana would call an "incident." Back in the kitchen, the voices are still going, but I can only hear bits and pieces of what Nana is saying.

"It just seems very sudden—"

"—I thought we were trying to work this whole thing out—"

"—Franny—"

I don't want to hear any more. I don't care what my uncle does. I get up and close my door.

CHAPTER 20

THE NEXT MORNING, UNCLE Gabe is sitting in the living room drinking coffee and looking at his phone. Across from him, Nana is in her usual spot on the sofa.

Uncle Gabe's big rolling suitcase is by the front door.

I go to the kitchen sink and drink a glass of water, the way Nana always likes me to do first thing in the morning. Then I grab a banana and put it in my backpack and go to the closet to get my boots and coat. While I'm doing all of this, my uncle and nana are watching. I feel like now I know what it's like to be on a stage.

And, unlike Mom, I don't enjoy it.

I guess that's one way we aren't alike.

"So, I'm taking off this morning," Uncle Gabe says as I'm putting on my coat. "Like we talked about last night."

We talked about it? Uh, okay then!

"Wish me luck with Mely." He holds up crossed fingers.

"What are we going to do?" I ask.

"You and me? We'll stay in touch for sure."

"Not you and me. I meant *Nana and me*." I watch his stupid

smile fade away. "Groceries and cooking and getting to places. All that stuff you came to help us with. What are we going to do about that?"

"All those things are doable online. Your nana can order groceries, she can get food delivered, she can get an Uber. All she has to do is spend a little money. Besides, she's going to be out of that wheelchair today."

"Unless the doctor finds something wrong we don't know about," Nana says.

"Nothing is going to go wrong," my uncle says. "You two need to stop with the guilt trip. I've been here almost two months. I need to get home. I get the message—you're mad. But this is all going to work out, you'll see. My Uber's going to be here any minute. How about a hug?"

I loop my scarf around my neck. "No."

"You're not going to give me a freaking hug goodbye?"

"Gabriel." Nana sounds tired, like it's the end of a long day instead of super early in the morning. "Leave her alone."

AT LEAST SCHOOL IS the same as always. Maybe it isn't so bad to have some things that don't change. Just like usual, I turn in my homework, turn my attention to the whiteboard, turn around in my seat, do whatever the teachers tell me to do. Just like usual, I head to the cafeteria and wait in line to get my lunch.

I sit down at the table, where Ruben and Tate are deep in discussion about some bit of *Silmarillion* trivia.

Arun and Eliot are eating quietly, not saying anything, even though I know they're both huge Tolkien nerds. That's when I know for sure they're just as sick of Tate as I am.

I pop open my milk. "Can we *please* talk about something else?"

Ruben says, "Hey! Don't yuck my yum, okay?"

Dr. Yao taught us to say this to each other. It's one of our old jokes. I have to laugh, and Ruben does too, and I think we're on the verge of being okay again when Tate speaks up.

"Just because you haven't read *The Silmarillion*, we're not supposed to talk about it? Who put you in charge? Calm down."

"Why don't *you* calm down, Tate?" I know I snap those words out, but I can only take so much in one day.

He leans over the table to pat my hand—yeech—and puts on a look of great fake concern. "Franny, maybe you need a break. You don't want to totally *lose it*."

It's not the words so much; it's how Tate says them. In a way that sounds significant.

Ruben's grin vanishes. He gets this weird, weak smile that's totally unlike him. And Arun and Eliot are staring down at their plates.

As a matter of fact, no one is looking at me.

Then I get it.

I understand what Ruben must have done.

There aren't enough deep breaths in the world to let me keep sitting here with him and Tate.

I'M IN THE LIBRARY, staring out the window. I can't wait for school to be over. I can't wait to leave and start working on my new plan, which is to somehow never come back here again.

Maybe Tate is right. Maybe I *am* losing it.

Eliot and Arun sit down with me.

"There you are," Arun says. "I was thinking we'd have to check the girls' bathroom next. Are you okay?"

I'm so embarrassed at my pink face and neck, I don't even say the usual thing about my allergies.

Eliot says, "Tate Grady is a butt-munch."

I can't believe I just heard those words from Mr. Perfect, Straight-A Eliot.

Arun nods. "He totally is, Franny."

But I notice they don't ask me what Tate was talking about. Or why I got so upset. "Did Ruben tell you guys something about my mom?"

They hesitate, then nod at the same time. It really is like they're brothers from different mothers. Arun says, "We were at Ruben's after school yesterday with Tate. Playing this game called Evolution for extra credit in life sciences. It's kind of a cool game, actually—"

Eliot cuts in. "Then out of nowhere Ruben says, 'You guys want to hear something weird I found out?'"

"He *said* that?"

"We said sure and then he told us about your mom's, uh . . . bipolar thing." Arun looks so embarrassed, I feel myself turn pink all over again.

"It's called bipolar disorder," Eliot says.

"Sorry. Bipolar disorder. And he asked whether we knew about it. But he didn't say much more than that because Eliot called him out. He said something like, 'Hey, does Franny know you're telling people that? Did she say it was okay?'"

Does someone in Eliot's family have a mental illness too? I say, "Thanks, bruh."

"My mom's a psychiatrist, and I thought that's what she would say."

"And Ruben got it," Arun says. "Right away he looked like he wished he could claw it back, you know? But it was too late by then. Tate, you know him. He just thought it was funny. He thinks it's okay to joke about anything."

"I bet Ruben didn't tell anyone else, though," Eliot says.

"Not after what Eliot said!" Arun chips in.

Maybe Ruben didn't. But even if he didn't, there's nothing stopping Tate from telling everyone.

No one is at our house when I get home from school. Nana is at the doctor's.

If I were Ruben or Lucy, I'd probably sit down and finish my homework. But I'm going to have plenty of time to finish tonight anyway. It's going to be back to the same old, same old around here, just me and Nana listening to NPR and getting ready for another exciting evening of PBS.

I go downstairs.

The bed is stripped. The sheets and blankets are dumped on the floor. The TV is still there on top of the bureau in front of its big mirror. It's just a big black rectangle of emptiness against the mirror, which is also a rectangle reflecting emptiness.

Some chunks of rock Uncle Gabe picked up on our walks are still sitting on his bedside table. There's some basalt and quartz, and a piece of shale. I remember him telling me their names and where they came from. He told me we live close to a super-old mountain range called the Watchung Mountains, and a long time ago those mountains were volcanoes. Yup, there were volcanoes in New Jersey.

I guess these rocks weren't important enough for Uncle Gabe to pack up and take home. Or maybe he just doesn't want to remember anything about being here.

I pick up the biggest chunk of quartz and lift it over my head with both hands, like a cavewoman or something. And—before I can stop and think—I throw it right at the TV.

It lands with a smash and then bounces onto the floor with a thump.

The big blank rectangle has a dent in it, a little gray star right in its middle. For a second I think maybe that's all that's going to happen. Maybe the TV will even still work. And then the cracks start growing outward. They reach out in all directions, until the whole screen is covered in a silvery-gray spiderweb of cracks. A few pieces pop loose and fall onto Uncle Gabe's bureau.

Oh man.

Why did I do that?

For Nana, if there's anything worse than buying an expensive new TV for no reason, it would be destroying an expensive new TV for no reason.

Upstairs, I hear my nana call my name. She's back!

I come out slowly from Uncle Gabe's room and glance at the door going into the garage. I think about just running out that door and going somewhere, anywhere, instead of having to go upstairs and face Nana.

Maybe that's what Mom felt like when she finally got out of prison.

Maybe that's why she never came back.

I think about not saying anything. But Nana will know something is up. She's one of those adults who can always tell. She says she gets lots of practice with people lying at the dental office.

I go up as slowly as I can dawdle, which is one of Nana's words, but when I come out into the hallway she's standing there, waiting for me. Something about her is different, but because I only give her a quick glance, I can't figure it out right away.

"What's wrong?" Nana asks. "What happened?"

I take a deep breath. "IbrokeUncleGabe'sTV."

"Say it, again, slower."

"I broke Uncle Gabe's TV."

"You *broke* it? How?"

"I hit it with a rock."

I wait for Nana to ask what I was thinking, but she doesn't. She just looks at me, shifting her grip on her walker. And then I see what's different.

How could I not notice?

The wheelchair is gone! Nana is using a walker, and her broken leg is in a brace. It's just a little bent instead of sticking out straight!

"Nana, your leg!"

She smiles sadly. "I know."

I feel worse. We should be celebrating! Jumping around yelling! Well, I could be jumping anyway, and Nana could be yelling enough for both of us. And instead we're both standing here looking at each other.

Uncle Gabe ruins everything!

Except that he didn't. Not this time. He didn't smash his own TV.

I was the one who did that.

Nana goes on, "I was hoping we could go out for dinner to celebrate, but Gracie has to babysit her nephew tonight and I'm just not ready to try an Uber yet. I'm still figuring out how to fold this walker."

"We could get some food delivered," I say.

I wait for her to say that it's too expensive.

Instead she says, "That sounds like a really good idea."

CHAPTER 21

WE ORDER ITALIAN. IT'S going to be a while because the best Italian restaurant in our town is always crowded, even on a Tuesday. I fix us some Triscuits and cheese, and some orange juice for myself, and Nana has a can of seltzer. We sit down in the living room to wait, and we talk over what I did to the TV. It's easier than I expected because Nana isn't as mad as I thought she would be. She's calm about it.

"Aren't you mad?" I finally ask.

"I'm not happy," my nana says. "But I'm not surprised, either. Your uncle decides to pack up and take off with no notice, no time for you to get used to the idea, acts like it's no big thing. Of course that was going to be triggering for you."

"What does triggering mean?"

I kind of already know. I've heard that word for ages—in school assemblies, on TV, from counselors. But right now I want to know exactly what it means.

"Well, it's something that upsets you because it brings up feelings or memories that come from a difficult experience." Nana sips her drink. "What Uncle Gabe did was too much like what your mom did. You were angry at her, too. It was worse back then because you were too little to talk about it."

"We don't talk about it now," I hear myself say.

Nana pauses before she takes another sip of seltzer. "Franny, we are literally talking about it right now."

"Not really."

Nana puts down her can. I put down my orange juice. We face each other from our different corners of the sofa.

"Well, what is it you want to talk about?"

"Nana, is there something wrong with me?" I think about Uncle Gabe's smashed TV. Tate saying I might lose it. Ruben ignoring me. All the way back to me kicking Aiden in the butt and the way Mrs. Dixon used to look at me. "I think there's something wrong with me. That's why everyone keeps leaving. Because I'm a bad person."

"Frances!" Nana points at me. "I don't *ever* want to hear you say that about yourself. It doesn't make you a bad person to have a few problems. Your uncle Gabe left because he's being a self-centered jerk. Your mom left because her judgment was not right at the time. She made some terrible decisions and she got sent to prison. That had nothing to do with anything you did, honeybee. You were four years old. You had nothing to do with your mother's bad choices, the things she did when she . . . "

Nana hesitates. I wait for her to describe my mom in the usual ways.

When your mom wasn't doing so hot.

When your mom was unwell.

Instead she says, "When she was having one of her bad manic episodes."

Did my nana just say "manic episode"?

She hurries on. "I'm not making excuses for her. She abandoned you, and there were times she neglected you—you have every right to be angry about that. But your mom had a serious mental illness. She didn't enjoy it. She wasn't using it to get attention or get her way or be a pain." Nana looks far away. "I tried to explain that to your uncle, but he—"

I wait for her to say something like "He was too busy with that fancy new college of his."

Instead she says, "He wasn't ready to hear it, I guess."

"Why didn't someone help her?" I've asked Nana this question before, but I ask it anyway. Like the answer might be different this time.

"People tried. Your poppy and I tried. It can be hard to treat mental illness. When your mom was in a manic cycle, she felt great. She didn't think she needed any help. She was the genius with great ideas who didn't even need to sleep. Then, when she was depressed, she felt so terrible all she wanted to do was curl up on the sofa and stare out the window. We called that her down place."

"What did she feel so terrible about?"

"I don't know. She never wanted to talk about that. When I sued for custody of you, she didn't argue, and I thought that meant she could see the sense in it. But lately I wonder if your mom was in her down place. That might explain why she just went along. By the time she was feeling better, it was too late. I had custody."

"You mean Mom didn't want to give me up?"

Nana hesitates. "It was complicated, but . . . no. She didn't want to give you up, Franny."

There's been something tight inside me that I didn't even know was tight until right now, when it loosens and falls away.

"She wanted you with her. But she could tell you needed more stability. When she was getting close to release, she talked about you living with her again. I told her we'd have to see how things were going and your mom said it was bad enough having one parole officer, she wasn't going to have two, and one of them in her own family." Nana looks tired and old—but she still smiles.

I don't ask what happened after that because I already know. Mom didn't move back close to us after her release, and she didn't come see us. When the parole officer called to ask Nana where Mom was, we didn't know. Mom had disappeared, the parole officer had said. She was gone.

I take a deep breath. "Maybe Mom's doing better now."

Nana looks sharply at me. "Maybe she is. Maybe she's taking care of herself. I'd like that to be true."

I can tell she doesn't believe it.

I hear myself say, "I miss Mom sometimes."

"You do?"

I think about it. I really think about it. Long hair the color of caramels. Arms tight around me. A low voice humming along with "Lush Life." "Sometimes I do."

"Well, your mom loves you. You should never forget that."

A scraping sound comes from our door.

We stop talking to stare at it. That seems like a weird way to deliver our food. You know, most people ring the bell.

"What is that?" Nana says.

"I'll check." I start to get up.

"Stay there. I'll check." Nana reaches for her walker and starts the slow business of standing up. Before she can get on her feet, the door opens, letting a burst of freezing air into our living room.

It's Uncle Gabe. He puts his keys back into his pocket. He drags his suitcase into the living room and leaves it in the middle of the floor. (Of course.) Then he goes back to close the door and I hear the *snick* of it locking.

"Gabe?" Nana says at last. "What are you doing here? Was your flight canceled?"

Lucy and her family, they adopted their dog, Snickerdoodle,

from the pound. He was pretty old when he came home with them, and he was scared. I remember he peed in the corner all the time for a while because he was too scared to ask to go outside. The expression on my uncle's face reminds me of how Snickerdoodle looked back then: anxious. And unsure about whether he was truly welcome.

Uncle Gabe says, "I made a mistake."

Like everything isn't complicated enough already, the doorbell rings again. The food is here!

AT LEAST DEALING WITH the food gives me something to do. I set the table while Uncle Gabe sits with Nana on the sofa and tells his long, dumb story.

How he started feeling kind of sick on the plane over Pennsylvania, and at first he thought it was because of the nachos he had in the airport, but then he gradually started to realize it was something else.

How he started imagining what Mely would say when she found out he was back. How the first thing she would say would be "So how is your mom doing?" and what she would say after that when she found out he'd come back earlier than planned.

How when he landed in Milwaukee he had to wait for his bag and then drag it up to the ticket counter and buy a ticket back to Newark Airport.

"And it was so expensive!" Uncle Gabe complains, like this is our fault somehow.

And then he had to get on another plane and fly back. By the time he finishes, the humble expression has left his face and he's just sitting there smiling like he's the best uncle ever. To me, it's more like he's just described the plot of a really stupid movie.

Then he says, I swear, "I'm hungry."

Nana says, "Well, I'm sorry. I got linguini with clams and I know you hate that. But Franny has a plain pizza."

She gives me one of those encouraging looks. A "be nice to your uncle" look.

I guess I'm supposed to jump up and grab a plate and set another place and ask Uncle Gabe what he would like to drink. Well, I don't say anything. I start eating. I'm not looking at my uncle.

The silence that falls is awkward.

I'm not just mad that he's back. I'm mad because Nana and I were finally having a good talk about Mom, and he interrupted it, and then wanted to be treated like some kind of big hero. Or just a good guy. He isn't either one!

When I come into the kitchen the next day for breakfast, Uncle Gabe is already there.

He's almost never up before me. He also never sits in the

kitchen with his coffee. He usually takes it back downstairs to drink while he's checking his emails. But here he is today, in his flannel pants and T-shirt, scratching his stomach.

There's no sound but my Cheerios rattling down into a cereal bowl and then a drawer opening and closing while I find a clean spoon.

Uncle Gabe finally clears his throat. "You may be interested to know that the TV was under a ninety-day unconditional warranty."

It takes me a moment to remember why he's talking about the TV. So much has been going on around here.

"What's that mean, an unconditional warranty?"

"That means that the store has to replace it, no matter why it quit working. Even if some irrational person smashed its screen with a baseball bat."

"It was a rock," I hear myself say.

I try to think of what to add to this, but I can't settle on anything. So I pour my milk and sit down to eat.

"That's all you have to say? You know, you're being a real little brat right now. To be honest, you're reminding me of your mom."

I know that's not a compliment.

It never is.

I blink hard. "Mom had some good points. You can ask Nana, or Carlton, if you don't believe me. She would never do what you did—say she was going to come and help and then just leave because she got *bored*."

My uncle's face is infuriatingly calm. "Give me a break. Your mom did whatever bizarre thing she felt like doing, usually."

Oh. It's *on*. "She did not! And she wasn't bizarre!"

"Uh, Franny? How would you know? You don't remember her."

"I do too! That bedspread you had on your bed when you got here? We had a bedspread just like that, one place we stayed. I remember it."

"Those are false memories." Uncle Gabe slurps his coffee. "Do some research. Look it up on the Internet. False memories aren't unusual. People want to remember something. So they do."

Can this be true? From the smug, satisfied look on his face, I think it must be. "Well, at least she had an excuse for being weird sometimes—she has bipolar!"

Uncle Gabe's eyes get huge when I say "bipolar."

That is not a word you hear spoken in our house. Until just lately.

"*You* don't have bipolar. You're just a big baby." Someone else is running my mouth. Someone who wants to insult him the way he just insulted Mom. "And you know what? I bet Mely knows that too! I bet she can see right through you! Why don't you just get on a plane again and go back home! Because Nana and I were fine before you got here and we'll be fine once you're gone! We don't need you!"

"What is going on out here?" Nana is in the hall, leaning on her walker. "The two of you, giving me agita at this time in the morning!"

"Your granddaughter has a major-league mouth on her, Ma."

Nana shakes her head and hop-hops toward the coffee maker. "I wonder who she got that from."

I WALK TO SCHOOL angry at my uncle. I don't even look around me while I walk, or stop to take any pictures. I just stomp along, muttering things I wish I had said.

My school comes into view. It's so early, there's just one kid sitting on the bench out front where Lucy and I used to sit sometimes.

Wait. Wait a moment.

Red hair.

Black cap.

I don't recognize the coat. But it's the kind Lucy wears, a big puffy ski jacket.

I give up on all this dumb, slow walking and break into a run.

CHAPTER 22

YOU SCARED THE CRAP out of me!" Lucy laughs and hands me another tissue. She's the kind of person who always has one of those little Kleenex packs.

I laugh too. "Why should a little crying scare *you*?"

My tears are all done now. When we hugged each other, that's when they came. They were like a cloudburst—a lot of rain, but over soon.

"You're always saying that it's healthy for people to cry," I remind Lucy.

"But you *never* do. Are you okay?"

I don't want to get into explaining everything that's been going on lately, not right now. I just say, "I was so surprised to see you."

"I almost started crying myself from fear!"

We laugh.

I wipe my nose one last time and then stuff the damp tissue ball into my coat pocket. "Okay, explain why you're back. You were supposed to be gone till the end of summer!"

"It's Gran's fault," Lucy says.

Of all the things Lucy and her family did that annoyed Gran, and it was a long list, the thing that annoyed Gran the most was Finn's hair. Finn's hair is the same color as Lucy's, but longer, way down past his shoulders. It's always been that way. He just likes having long hair. But their gran hated it.

"She kept saying it wasn't a proper little boy's haircut," Lucy tells me.

And then Lucy's family went to somewhere called the Cotswolds to visit some friends for the weekend. Finn had a cold, so they left him with Gran, who said it was no problem.

"And the reason it was no *problem*," Lucy says dramatically, "was because the day we left, Gran bribed Finn with a movie and Maccy's if he'd go get his hair cut!"

"Maccy's" is what Lucy and her brothers call McDonald's. And they never get it, which only makes them want it more.

"Finn will do *anything* for Maccy's, so he went along with it. But the second the haircut was over, Finn went *ballistic*. He started crying and wouldn't stop. Gran finally had to call Mum and ask her what to do because Finn wouldn't calm down. And when Mum found out what Gran had done, *Finn* wasn't the only one who went ballistic. Mum and Dad had a mega row about it. Dad said we needed to make allowances for Gran because she's from a different generation and sees things differently. Mum said that was total *codswallop* and that Gran is just a hateful old control freak."

I store the word "codswallop" away.

"And then she told us to pack up and we were on a plane here the *next day*. Dad's still back in London. He and Mum aren't really talking. And Mum and Gran aren't talking *at all*." Lucy wrinkles her forehead.

"Are you okay?"

"Only, I'm a bit worried about the argument. I've *never* heard them yell at each other that way before. And we haven't heard from Dad since we left. He usually calls every day when we're not all together. Don't tell anyone, okay?"

"I won't."

"I'm afraid he's still angry at us for leaving."

I think of some of the things we've said recently in *my* house. Like, just this morning. "I think adults fight sometimes and it's normal. Uncle Gabe and Nana do, all the time."

I can't believe I'm offering advice on family relationships to Lucy Bernal, but here I am doing it.

"Hey, Lucy—" I say.

She sits up. Her eyes get big. "You have a new best friend," she blurts out.

"What?! No!"

"I was so afraid you'd make one while I was away."

"Seriously?" I poke her and she pulls away, laughing. Lucy is super ticklish. "Who could replace the Loolybird? I was mainly hanging out with Ruben. But now he has this new friend who I can't stand. Tate Grady?"

"Oh, I know Tate. Sometimes he's okay, but it's like he can never *stop* showing off. It's so annoying."

She always says the right thing. It's like magic.

I look around. It's still quiet out here, and it'll be like that until the buses start pulling in. I remind myself that Lucy and Ruben are not much alike. "Lucy, you know about my mom, right?"

Lucy looks a little surprised. She knows some things about Mom. Not as many deets as Ruben, mainly because she's always too polite to ask. She nods.

I tell Lucy, "She has, um, bipolar."

I'm surprised at how calm she stays. "Wow, I'm sorry. I know that can be hard."

And then she shocks me.

"My aunt Hilary has that."

I know Lucy's aunt Hilary. She visits them sometimes. She has freckles and she knits. That sounds basic, but she makes Lucy the most amazing sweaters. And she has a job and friends and her own apartment. I guess what I mean is that she's like any other grown-up.

"Really?" I say. "When did she know she had it?"

"I think she was in her twenties or something. It was hard

for a while. She had to take a break from university. But they got her on the right meds, and she sees her psychiatrist every week, and she's fine."

Lucy shrugs. Like her aunt's bipolar is no big deal. I feel a twinge of jealousy, so sharp that it almost hurts. It must be nice to be Lucy.

"Is *that* why your mum isn't around?" she asks.

I nod. "I guess Mom won't admit there's anything wrong. I mean, she will sometimes. But when she starts feeling better, she stops taking her meds and goes back to saying she doesn't have a problem. Nana said if Mom wanted to see us, she had to be in treatment. So Mom doesn't see us."

I let myself feel sorry and sad. As sad as I want, for once.

"We don't even know where she is now," I mumble.

Lucy puts her arm around me. We sit for a while like that.

"Listen, Franny. Mum says I can't have a friend over until I'm unpacked, but I think I can get that done by tomorrow. Do you want to come over Friday after school? We can talk more about all this." Then she adds, in her perfect Lucy way, "Or we can talk about something *else* if you want."

"I think so. I just have to ask Nana."

"See you at lunch?" Lucy asks. I have time to nod before another of Lucy's friends spots her and rushes over to say hi.

AFTER SCHOOL I ASK Nana about going to Lucy's. She says, "That's fine. But you need to be back by five to help me with dinner. Someone's coming over on Friday night."

"Who's coming to dinner?"

"That's a surprise."

I can tell by the way Nana says it that I'm not getting any more out of her and it's useless to try.

If it's Aunt Gracie, and she's bringing food, I just hope she remembers I'm a vegetarian.

CHAPTER 23

FRIDAY NIGHT, NANA INSISTS on setting the table herself. She's pulled it out from the wall and she's moving around it slowly with her walker. The desk chair from my bedroom is there. Five chairs altogether. That means we're having two guests.

"I think this might have actually been easier with my wheelchair. I guess it'll take me a while to get used to something new." She stops and laughs. "And then it'll be time for it to change again!"

The doorbell rings and Nana goes slowly across to open it. There's Aunt Gracie with two big takeout bags.

I go to help Aunt Gracie. I wonder who our other dinner guest is. I'm guessing one of Nana's other dental office friends. I hope it's Amethyst. She always smells great and gives the best hugs and she never asks me what my favorite subject in school is.

The bags are full of sushi. We don't have that very often. It looks like someone's pulled out the stops with a credit card today!

"I got Franny the Vegetarian Special," Aunt Gracie says. "And there's seaweed salad, too."

"Thanks, Aunt Gracie."

"I'm going to go check the bathroom," Nana says.

She's off to make sure our toilet's working okay. We haven't had any more serious problems, but Nana calls it "temperamental." "Like everyone else around here," she adds sometimes.

I keep my voice low. "Aunt Gracie? I'm sorry I called you Aunt Gravy that time. It was super rude. And thanks for not snitching me out to Nana. She would have been mad."

She keeps her voice quiet too. "Thank you. I appreciate that. But why 'Aunt Gravy'? Where did you come up with that?"

"You used to smell like gravy a lot." It sounds so dumb to say out loud. "You don't nearly as much anymore, though."

"Hmm. Well, I made a lot of meals in my slow cooker, because I worked full-time. Joe, my late husband, used to say everything you make in a slow cooker tastes like gravy after a while. And Chester used to just love meat chunks in rich gravy, and that probably didn't help either."

"Just put everything out on the counter, and people can help themselves." Nana's back, kicking one of my uncle's socks out of sight under the sofa. She still can't bend over and get things easily.

Since my uncle returned, he's barely spending any time upstairs, but somehow his crap is still all over the place.

The doorbell rings again.

"Franny, can you get that?"

Carlton is on our stoop with a massive bakery box and a shoulder bag.

He stands there looking nervous. I'm so surprised, I can't move, and I guess that eases his nervousness. Because then he laughs and says, "How are you doing? Can I come in?"

"For heaven's sake, let the man in. It's cold," Nana says. "Oh my God! Is that box for us?"

"I couldn't come with my arms hanging, my mom would never forgive me," Carlton says, putting the bags down on the side table and taking off his jacket. "How are you doing, Mrs. Petroski? Thanks so much for the invite."

Nana called him?!

"Call me Andi, Carlton. You look great. This is my old friend Grace Hutchins—we worked at the same dental practice. What would you like to drink?"

There's even some wine that Uncle Gabe didn't buy!

I take a peek in the pastry box while I'm putting it on the counter. Rainbow cookies, mini cannoli, pignoli, struffoli. Oh my gosh, my favorite, sfogliatelle! I wish we could have dessert right away. But first we have to have dinner with all the boring adult talk about jobs and health stuff and what everyone over in Livingston has been doing for the last twenty years or whatever. Uncle Gabe says almost nothing. I think he's as surprised to see Carlton here as I am.

After dinner the adults get coffee and I get a cup of

224

peppermint tea and finally a sfogliatella. We all sit in the living room. Uncle Gabe too. The adult chatter dies away. Carlton turns to me and says, "So, Franny, I'm leaving for LA in a few days."

He catches me with a mouthful of pastry and all I can do is nod and make an encouraging noise that makes everyone laugh.

"But before I left, I wanted to make sure I gave you this, and I wanted to tell you it was great to see you again."

He opens the shoulder bag and lays a couple of things on the coffee table.

One memory stick.

And a manila envelope.

It's not sealed. I can see the flap is loose.

I look over at Nana. She raises her eyebrows and nods. I wipe my hands on my pants and pick up the envelope. I'm nervous, so I fumble, and then bunches of shiny pictures slide out.

These are family pictures.

There's a picture of me, Mom, and Nana in a dim little room that I think might be that apartment in Somerville, and another one that's me, Mom, Nana, and Poppy standing in front of some trees. But most of the pictures are of me, or of Mom and me.

There's me eating spaghetti on the floor. I'm sitting on a blue plastic sheet, like we use in Studio Club, making a huge mess. There's Mom and me asleep on a sofa. Walking in a park. Sitting at a big table with a bunch of grinning adults I don't know. While I look through the pictures, I catch some of what Carlton is saying.

"You loved spaghetti, it was your favorite. . . . You always ate on the floor, your mom thought high chairs were bougie. . . . That was right after you and your mom moved out to Quincy. . . . That was on Boston Common right before this concert your mom sang in. . . . That was at this big Thanksgiving dinner your mom and I had, with all our friends from back then. . . . "

In the beginning I'm just a baby and my hair is like dandelion fluff and waving all around my head and then it gets more like the color of butter and starts flattening down.

I can't believe I finally have all these pictures of Mom and me. Like we were a real family.

Then I stop flipping to stare at one picture. Carlton leans over to take a look. I can tell he thinks it's nothing special. Just me sitting on a bed in some apartment somewhere.

"That was right before I left Boston for Philly," Carlton says.

"Uncle Gabe," I say.

My uncle looks surprised that I'm talking to him. I turn the picture around so he can see it.

"Look at the bedspread," I tell him.

It's a candlewick bedspread, like the one in his room.

Uncle Gabe looks at it, then back at me. I can tell he knows why I'm showing him the picture. Then he surprises me. "You were right. I was wrong."

False memory, my butt.

I turn over the last picture in the stack. It's me sitting on someone's stoop by myself. I'm older. My hair is down to my shoulders, and, wow, is it snarled. My hands are tucked under my legs like I'm cold, even though I'm in shorts and a tank top, so it must be summer.

"That was my old apartment in Philly," Carlton said. "That was the day your mom dropped you off with me. She wanted a picture of you to take with her. She kept telling you to smile, but you wouldn't."

"*You* were the friend Mom left me with?"

"That was me." He leans over for a better look. "She thought it would be okay to leave you with me because we knew each other. Uncle Carlton, remember?" Carlton draws a long breath. "You weren't happy. I guess you can tell from that picture. The first day, you didn't want to talk to me, and you wouldn't eat, either. You just wanted to sit on the floor and listen to your mom's records."

"She left them with us?"

I catch Carlton's look of surprise as he glances at Nana. "You didn't know that? Your mom could tell you were kind of scared, and not too happy. So she left her records with you. She told you that when you listened to them, it would be like she was there too. And you needed to keep them safe for her because she'd be back soon. Do you remember her saying that?"

Mom meant to come back for me. She'd never have left her records if she wasn't going to come back. And she didn't just dump me with some rando, either. She left me with Carlton.

"But she had a plan to execute first. A plan to make some money and get you guys back into your own place."

Uncle Gabe says, "Doing some favors for her lit new friends."

"I never said it was a *good* plan," Carlton says.

I'm not going to let the adults sidetrack this. "So what happened then?"

"Well, you were supposed to be with me for a few days, and then it was a few days more. Your mom was super excited when we talked. Maybe you remember the way she could get. Everything was going great, couldn't be better, she just needed a little more time. It was a week and then it was going on for two weeks."

I think I might remember a little of that. Mom all excited, talking fast.

"Finally I said she needed to come back and get you. I was waiting tables then—I couldn't have you in a booth in the restaurant for six hours straight, and I couldn't leave you with the landlady every night either. Your mom said it would just be a few more days. I said, no, not just a few more days. Then she lost her temper."

I can see Carlton swallow.

"She said some things. I said some things—things that I really wish I could take back. That was the last time we talked."

I look down at the picture. It's hard hearing stories like these about Mom.

Then Nana says, "And now we finally get to the part of the story that's interesting."

Even Uncle Gabe laughs.

"Yes. That was when your nana entered the picture." Carlton turns to Nana. "I knew my mom would know where you were and how to get in touch with you. So I called her. Of course first I had to answer all kinds of questions about when I was coming to see her again and whether I was eating a salad every day, but after she was done with that, she gave me your phone number." He turns back to me. "I got in touch with your nana. She left right away and drove down to Philly to pick you up."

Wait.

"Nana *drove* to *Philly*?"

There is no way to get to Philly without driving on a busy highway with tons of big trucks going fast.

Nana says, "I had to, so I did it."

"And soon after that," my uncle says, "if I remember right, your mom took the train from Boston to Newark with a backpack to hand off to some friend of a friend and got arrested in his apartment."

Nana nods. "One of her wonderful new friends turned out to be a narc."

It's so weird hearing my grandmother say "narc."

Aunt Gracie says, "How about you, Gabe? Where were you while all this was going on?"

"Uh, I was in Madison. I had just gotten out of college."

"A lot of picnics and learning how to sail on Lake Mendota, as I recall." Nana's voice is dry.

"Actually, I was job hunting." Uncle Gabe's voice is just as dry as Nana's. Still, I notice he's studying the half-eaten cannoli on his plate like it's the most fascinating thing he's ever seen.

Aunt Gracie quickly asks Uncle Gabe about the winters in Wisconsin, and all the boring adult talk kicks in again. For once, I don't mind. I've got a lot to think about. While Uncle Gabe is describing what it's like to go ice fishing, Carlton leans over and whispers, "Every single picture I have of you and your mom is on that memory stick, by the way."

Wow. I know that must have taken a while.

"And I made a copy of it for myself, in case something happens to that one," he says. "So don't worry about that."

"Thanks" doesn't seem like enough.

I watch him fork a piece of cannoli into his mouth. I lick my lips. "Carlton, did you know my mom was—um, had a mental health disorder? She has bipolar."

It's still scary to tell people that, but I hope it's going to get easier.

He doesn't look surprised to hear the word "bipolar" and he doesn't look surprised that I asked, either. "Your nana told me when she came to pick you up in Philly. She and I had a long talk that day. I already knew something was going on, capeesh? I just didn't know what to call it. But us knowing it and convincing your mom to admit it and get help—those were two different things."

I think all that over. Then I ask, "Is it okay if I start calling you Uncle Carlton again?"

His smile practically splits his face in half. There's something familiar about it. I don't know—I think maybe I remember it from when I was little. "I would like that."

CHAPTER 24

SATURDAY IS A GOOD day. I look through my photos and start planning a scrapbook with family pictures in it, and Lucy and I go to the library in the afternoon.

But Sunday drags. I have to admit, I miss going to Ruben's.

Nana doesn't mention Game Day and I wonder if she's guessed Ruben and I had a fight.

Finally I decide to do something useful. The towels in our bathroom have gotten mega smelly, so I gather them up and take them downstairs.

When you hear adults complain about how much laundry they do, they're not lying. Take it from me—they have to do it *all the time*.

There's something big piled on top of the washer. It's the candlewick bedspread, all balled up. At first I think Uncle Gabe is acting like a baby again. But then I see there's a hole torn right down its front. I can't blame Uncle Gabe for that. The fabric there was worn thin already.

I rub the bedspread against my face. Maybe I'll hang on to it for a while. There's something about the nubbles I like.

Then I look over at the kite. That kite I dragged out of the bushes way back in January.

I look from it to the bedspread. From the bedspread to the kite. I do that for a while, while my art brain works away.

And then I take the kite and carry it over to the card table I've been using for my art projects. I grab Mr. Tan's tin that has the scissors in it.

I take the bedspread in my hands and tear it right down the middle. Then it's time to get out the scissors and start cutting strips.

A WHILE LATER I hear Nana's voice coming from far away.

I realize it's not the first time I've heard that voice this afternoon. I think I remember even calling back a few times. I've been down here awhile. I'm thirsty and hungry and I have to pee, bad.

I dash into Uncle Gabe's bathroom and when I come back out, I can hear a funny slithery sound from the stairs. One crutch, then another, skids down the steps and lands at the bottom.

Nana mostly uses the walker right now, but she's working on getting used to her crutches, too.

I hear a *thump, thump* sound.

I let myself give one frustrated sigh. I just needed a little more time. I was so close to being done!

I go over to the stairs and pick up the crutches.

The *thump, thump* is Nana coming down the stairs on her butt.

"Nana, what are you doing?"

"I'm coming to check on you. Dinner is almost ready!"

I scold Nana the way she scolds me. "You should have had Uncle Gabe come down."

"He's busy cooking. What have you been doing? You've been down here for hours."

I help Nana up and get the crutches under her arms and stay close, but not too close, as she does her hop-hop over to the kite thing.

Most of the black plastic has been covered over with cloth, although you can still see some of its dusty edges. I put on layers of the candlewick bedspread in all kinds of ways. Some of it is stapled, some of it is sewn on, and the last of it is glued. The bedspread worked well because it's nubbly, and textured stuff is always good. Then when I had enough bedspread, I started building up layers of other things. There are pieces from Mom's old skirt and her long pink tunic with the stain on the front. There are long strips I cut from Nana's worn-out work scrubs. There are patches from my yellow shirt I'd ruined with ink spatters in art class. (I forgot my smock that day. Nana was ticked.) And some of Mr. Tan's wild-colored socks from the rag bag.

Some of the cloth is scrunched up, some of it dangles off.

A few strips reach practically to the floor. It's almost like the kite is changing from one thing to another but isn't there yet.

My favorite part is the tail. I braided the original black plastic with pieces of Mom's clothes and pieces of Nana's clothes. And whenever any of the three parts started getting short, I just tied on more cloth strips to keep them going. The tail got really, really long before I decided it was done and tied it off with a strip of my yellow shirt, the way you'd tie off a braid with a ribbon.

I didn't trim any ragged edges. I left all the knots big and bulky. I did it all my way. Petroski style.

I know it isn't done and maybe it isn't any good at all, but I kind of like it.

Nana touches one of the pieces from Mom's tunic and then looks around until she spots the purple duffel bag. It's not like I hid it or anything. It's just gaping open on the floor. Her gaze travels from the duffel to Mom's portable record player on the shelf next to the washing machine.

"Nana, I went in your room—" I start.

Nana puts up her hand to shush me. "I should have given you these things a long time ago."

She's back to looking at the kite. She touches one dangling strip of bright pink cloth.

I say, "That tunic had a big stain, so I didn't think anyone would want it. And that's my shirt with the ink on it, and those are your old scrubs. It's all got to dry. I used tons of glue."

Come to think of it, the whole basement reeks of glue. Next time I should remember to open the door to the garage.

Nana says, "We're all in here, Franny. Your mom, me, and you."

I hadn't thought of that.

There are all these different kinds of cloth from all kinds of different people that clash but also go together. Not just our family. Mr. Tan and his socks, too.

"You need to take this to school. You can have it in the Open House, right? It's not too late?"

I shake my head. Nana keeps on surprising me. If you'd asked me yesterday, I would have said she didn't even know the Open House was coming up.

All I can think to say is "It needs to dry more before I take it to school."

The kite thing is pretty damp and sticky.

"Put the fan on it. It'll dry a lot faster. I bet it'll be ready tomorrow morning. I hope so anyway! There's a *lot* of glue on this thing!"

I have to laugh. "It was the only way."

"Well, you should know, honeybee." Nana puts her arm around me. "You're the artist."

THE NEXT MORNING, UNCLE Gabe gives me and the kite a ride to school.

I can see him looking over the kite while we're loading it into the back seat. He doesn't say whether he likes it, but he hasn't been saying much of anything since Carlton's visit.

The smell of glue is still strong. My uncle rolls down his window.

The ride is silent until he says, "So, the new TV is coming today."

Just hearing the word "TV" is embarrassing. I give one quick nod.

"I'm going to ask them to put it upstairs this time. That way we can all watch it. It still isn't easy for your nana to get in and out of the basement."

I say, "Are you sure Nana's going to like that?"

"She'll be okay with it."

You know what? I think he's right. It won't be a big deal now.

I sneak a look at him. "It's going to be kind of weird, all of us hanging out in the living room."

"Maybe it won't be so weird by the time I leave again. Maybe we'll get used to it."

"Are you going to stay?"

Uncle Gabe pulls the car into the teachers' parking lot and scores a spot by the back entrance. He leaves his blinkers on to show it's only temporary. "If something changes, I'll make sure to talk it over with you and Ma. I won't spring it on you again the way I did."

I hope he means it.

"I've been thinking about why I left. Why I'd leave people who wanted me around, and needed me, to go be with someone who doesn't really want me around. And doesn't need me anymore." He clears his throat. "Franny, being your mom's little brother, it wasn't easy for me. All the time, hearing 'Your sister did this' or 'Your sister said that.' I couldn't wait to get away to college, away from all that mess, all that drama that just never stopped. Even when Ma told me Mia wasn't doing well, I couldn't come back and face it again."

He's talking without looking at me.

"I didn't go see your mother in prison. Not once. Mely thought that was awful. I didn't want to come back to New Jersey this time either. I think I did it to impress Mely. To show her I had turned into a stand-up guy. But it's been good getting to know you. You're a cool kid. I like that you do your own thing and don't worry too much about what other people think."

I'm not sure that's true, but I like thinking it could be true. I make up my mind to be more like that person Uncle Gabe just described.

"Even seeing Ma again feels right. That doesn't mean it's always easy. But—I shouldn't have left the way I did. That was stupid. I won't spring it on you again like that. I promise."

He finally turns to face me.

I say what I've needed to say for a while. "I'm sorry about what I did to your TV."

Then a horn blasts loudly behind us and makes us both jump.

Mr. Winkler is sitting in his car, glaring through the windshield. He opens his door and shouts, "Excuse me! This is the *teachers'* parking lot!"

CHAPTER 25

THAT NIGHT, NANA AND I eat dinner together because Uncle Gabe has a deadline. At first I thought he might be fibbing because we're having lentil soup. (It's not his favorite.) But when I went downstairs to check on him, his door was closed, his keyboard was clacking, and Black Flag was playing. So I guess he actually is working and it's not just an excuse to sneak out to Taco Bell later.

It's okay. There's something I wanted to talk to Nana about anyway. "Nana, I told some of my friends about Mom's bipolar."

It used to be that whenever I brought up Mom, Nana would look old and worried. Not tonight. She looks calm. "How did they take it?"

"Mostly okay." There's no way I'm telling her what Ruben did. I think she might call Dr. Yao, and Franny Petroski is not a snitch, even when someone kind of deserves it. "You're not mad?"

"There's a difference between privacy and secrecy. Privacy is okay. People are entitled to keep stuff about their personal lives to themselves. Secrecy is not so okay, because it's usually motivated by shame and fear. I always thought I was being private about your mom, but maybe I was being secretive. That wasn't so good for you. Or for me."

Adults.

Are they allowed to just change the rules anytime they want?

Nana gives her snort of a laugh.

Oh man! I think I said that out loud.

Nana says, "You want me to have all the answers, but there are some things I'm still figuring out. Even if I am an adult. Sorry about that."

Well, okay, but adults are *supposed* to have the answers. That's why they're adults and they get to make the rules and we kids aren't and don't.

"Do you think I'm going to be like Mom?"

Nana knows what I'm getting at. "Are you asking whether you're going to have bipolar?"

I nod and wait for her to reassure me, the way she did when I asked whether Mom was dead.

Instead Nana says, "I don't know, honeybee. It does run in families. The average age of onset is something like twenty-five. Looking back, I know your mom had symptoms much earlier than that. You don't remind me all that much of your mom when she was your age. Except for your creativity—the way it comes so easy to you. That confidence you have in it. But I can't say you won't develop bipolar, because we don't know yet."

"What'll we do if I get it?"

Nana sighs. "Hopefully you'll be able to admit you have a problem. If you can do that, everything else is easier. We'll deal with it. It might not be fun, but, Frances Ella, think of all the hard things we've done together already. We're a good team."

I push away my half-empty bowl of soup.

My nana says, "You know, it's very common for kids with mentally ill parents to worry that they'll inherit their parent's disorder."

I didn't know that. I guess it helps a little.

Nana puts her elbows on the table, the way she does when she's done eating. "When I hurt my knee, I was really frightened. I felt so alone. But then your aunt Gracie pointed me to that support group for people with knee injuries. We were all in the same place and we all wanted to help each other. And it was great."

Nana, I know all that, I say in my head.

I'm pretty sure I say it out loud!

But Nana just keeps on talking.

"Somehow in our group chats the subject of mental illness came up. And for the first time in ages I was telling people about your mom. What it was like being her parent. Feeling like her mental illness must be our fault. Worrying about her all the time. Then worrying about *you* all the time. Well, some of my knee injury friends have similar issues in their families."

"Really?"

Nana nods. "Mental illness is a lot more common than people

might think. It's just that no one ever talks about it. We've formed our own little support group now, and it's changed my life."

Nana clears her throat in an embarrassed way. Those words are dramatic coming from her, and I know how Nana and Uncle Gabe feel about drama.

I knew something had happened with Nana. I just knew it!

"Maybe we could look for a group like that for you."

I think it over. "Is there something like that?"

"As a matter of fact, I called Dr. Aronfeld to ask that same question, and she's running a weekly support group for kids with mentally ill family members. Remember Dr. Aronfeld?"

I used to see Dr. Aronfeld when I was in elementary school. She let me talk about anything I wanted, and if I didn't want to say anything, I could just draw or play. And we always had a snack before I left, which was my favorite part. But then there was some problem with our insurance.

"She got too expensive," I remind Nana.

"You let me worry about that."

I hesitate and Nana gives me a concerned look. But I'm not pausing for the reason she thinks. "Eliot's mom is a psychiatrist. Maybe she knows about some groups too."

"That's a good idea." Nana pushes the bread over to me. "Have a slice. You've barely eaten anything."

I take a piece of bread and dunk it in my soup. It's still warm, which is nice. Because all of a sudden I'm hungry again.

CHAPTER 26

I'M STANDING BY MY display at the Studio Club Open House, the way Miss Midori asked us to. That way we can answer any questions or just talk to people who might be curious about what we made.

Mostly people ask me whether it's okay to pick up the *Milk Jug Emergency Room* and look inside. Or whether they can touch the big knots in my weaving. Even though I have a sign saying, "It's Okay to Touch These Pieces!" There's one boy who jokes about going through the recycling bin in his house and making some art. I tell him he totally should.

Most of the kids and teachers have come through by now. Ruben and Tate didn't stop to look at my stuff. They just walked by. Which hurt my feelings, but maybe it's better this way.

Whatever. It's quieted down, and I decide to make a quick trip to the bathroom.

When I come out, someone says, "Hey, Franny."

I jump about a foot in the air before I see it's Ruben.

"I just wanted to talk to you for a second." He twists his hands together, like he does when he's nervous. "To say I'm sorry for telling people about your mom."

Sometimes you're so mad at someone, you think you'll never get over it, and then they say those two words, "I'm sorry," and things are better right away. Maybe not great, but they can help. A lot.

"Why did you do that? You said you wouldn't!"

"I don't know why. I kept wondering whether you'd told anyone else about it. Like, maybe I was the only person who didn't know? And I was kind of mad at you too. About the—"

"I know, I know. The social-skills joke."

"I haven't told anyone else though. Except for Reyna."

"Reyna?"

"She wanted to know why you weren't coming to Game Day anymore. She wouldn't leave me alone about it. Then, once I told her what had happened, she said she couldn't believe I blabbed about something like that. She said even I should have better sense. That I should never have told anyone if you asked me not to."

Reyna doesn't even like me, I say in my head.

Only as usual I manage to say it out loud.

"Come on, Reyna doesn't like me, either. I'm not sure she likes anyone right now except for a few of the girls on her basketball team. But that doesn't matter. I knew she was right."

Ruben scratches his head. "So, like I said, I'm sorry. If it helps, I know Arun and Eliot won't tell anyone. And I told Tate not to say anything either. He said he hadn't. He said to tell you he was just trying to be funny that day at lunch. He didn't know it would bug you so much." Ruben waits to see what I make of that.

What I think is there's a difference between saying you were just trying to be "funny" and really apologizing.

But Tate's Tate. I already know that, and I also know that nothing I say is going to change Ruben's mind about him.

We walk back into the auditorium together.

Ruben says, "Hey, by the way, I like your kite. Now I get why you saved it. I can't believe that's the same thing we found out in the bushes."

"I know. But it isn't really the same thing we found, right? It's something else now."

"I guess that's true. It's cool, anyway."

Ruben looks around to see where Tate is. He's going to spot him and take off in a second. Before he can, I say, "Hey, Rubes, did I tell you we got a new TV?"

"What happened to the old one?" Ruben is still a fan of the old technologies.

"We put it in the basement, don't worry. Nana says it's probably a valuable antique. You should come over sometime and we could watch a movie or whatever. On the *new* TV," I emphasize.

"That would be cool." Ruben hesitates. "I heard Arun is having some people over for cards this weekend. You going?"

I nod. I don't ask whether Ruben will be there. I already know Arun asked him and Ruben said he was busy.

Ruben waves and goes to catch up with Tate and I walk back to my art pieces.

I ended up sticking lots of different objects on the front of the kite thing. Some big buttons from one of Nana's old-fashioned cloth coats. Some used-up, squished-out tubes of oil paint from my art box, one of my favorite Yayoi Kusama postcards (*Pumpkins Screaming About Love Beyond Infinity*). There are some of the shards from Uncle Gabe's broken TV that weren't too sharp, and some of the bark pieces from the sycamore tree in Livingston. I ended up touching it up with some paint, too.

For Nana's sake.

But the lavender and blue streaks and splotches look good. They remind me of the way shadows have been looking in our town this winter, in the late afternoon when I'm walking home from school.

At first I called the kite thing *Found Object*.

Partly because almost everything in it is something I found or that someone else threw away.

And partly because lately I've been wondering whether Mom is kind of a found object too.

I know she did some bad things. But think about the way a lot of people talk about someone like her. A lot of them don't need to hear any more after they hear stuff like "prison" or "mental illness." It's like she got put in a dumpster too.

Well, I don't want to leave her in there anymore.

Even if I'm still deciding what I could do about it.

I ended up calling the kite project *Found Objects*. Which could apply to a lot of us.

I watch Nana hop-hopping around, looking at everyone's pieces. She's still slow, but faster every week. She can put more and more weight on her hurt leg. Her recovery is a work in progress, she says.

Uncle Gabe is wandering around too. On his own. It's been going okay with Nana and Uncle Gabe in the same house watching the same TV, but that doesn't mean they don't need breaks from each other. All that togetherness is coming to an end now because Uncle Gabe is going home this weekend. We're visiting him at Christmas. Nana is already muttering about how loopy it is to go to Wisconsin in December.

Yup, Nana's changed a lot. Uncle Gabe too. And me? I'm going to have to think about that. Maybe talk it over with the kids in my support group. I go once a week now because Aunt Gracie figured out how to make our insurance pay for it. It turns out she's good at that. Nana says she's going to unleash Aunt Gracie on the hospital next.

Miss Midori calls, "Okay, artists! Time to get that group photo!"

We all crowd down front, and I slip in next to Lucy. She grabs my hand. When Miss Midori calls "One—two—three—*Alexander Calder*!" we all jump as high as we can, and she takes the picture while everyone is in midair.

CHAPTER 27

AFTER THE OPEN HOUSE, Nana drives us to the diner. She's just started driving again and it's a slow trip. For some reason she stops on Valley Road, opposite our house. It's the same spot where Dr. Yao pulled over back in January, the first time we saw it. Now it's March and the snow is starting to droop, and green shoots are coming up in our yard. Nana says they're snowdrops.

She sits there, hands on the steering wheel at ten o'clock and two o'clock, peering at La Maison de la Plaque Dentaire like it's a place she's never seen before. "It might not be the most beautiful house, but I've gotten kind of attached to it. What do you think, Franny?"

"I like it."

I wouldn't say this to Nana, but the truth is I'm not looking forward to going back to the apartment. Not that it isn't fine, but I've gotten used to more room and our own washer and dryer. And the toilet's been behaving itself lately too.

At the diner, our usual waitress, Demetria, makes a huge fuss because she hasn't seen us in so long. Nana has to explain all about her knee, and then introduce Uncle Gabe. Finally we can order. Lamb chops for Nana, spanakopita for me. Uncle Gabe orders a burger with Greek fries, which come covered in feta cheese. After Demetria drops off our drinks, Nana says, "I've been thinking about something, and I'd like to talk it over with you two. I got a call from Dr. Yao a month or so ago."

I haven't seen Dr. Yao in what feels like ages. I miss her, but what can I do?

"She told me Mr. Tan and his family have decided to sell the house," Nana says.

Oh man. I start calculating how to squeeze all my art materials and projects back into our old apartment. Maybe I could just make my bedroom into an art space and sleep in the living room. Ha! I already know Nana's not going to go for that.

"What's so funny, honeybee?" Nana asks.

"I was just thinking about how I'm going to fit all my art supplies back into the apartment."

"That's something I've been thinking about too. I know how much you love having that space for your work. I like having a yard. And I'd like to be able to paint the walls or get a cat without having to ask a landlord first. So I'm wondering whether we should buy La casa.de placa dental."

A cat?

A house?!

I must be dreaming or something.

Across from us, Uncle Gabe stops slurping his milkshake, so I can tell he's surprised too.

"That sounds expensive," I say at last.

"It's not too bad if we take the house as is. Mr. Tan's family really doesn't want the hassle of cleaning his things out or making repairs. They'll give us a break on the price if they don't have to do that. But that means we'll be dealing with everything—all that junk in the basement, kitten pictures, exploding toilets, you name it. We'll have our work cut out for us. Gabe, what do you think?"

"It sounds like it might be a good deal. I've been telling you for years that buying usually makes better financial sense than renting."

"I wasn't ready. I have a lot of anxiety about spending large amounts of money. Gracie told me that I should go ahead and make a bid and I practically tore her head off. But the more I think about it, the more I think it's a good idea. I think we can manage." This is the way she talks sometimes now. Like Mr. Burns. Nana's support groups are rubbing off on her.

Who am I to judge people about anxiety? I think of all those lists I drew up of Things Currently Worrying Franny Petroski. I haven't made a new one in ages. Did I just get too busy? Do things feel like they're under better control now? Maybe it's that Nana and I made it through the knee thing together. If we can do that, we can do a lot of other things, too, even things that are scary.

～⌒～

AT NINE O'CLOCK, AS usual, Nana taps on my bedroom door and waits for me to say "Come in" before she does. "Your phone?"

I look up from my magazine, an old *Artforum* from Miss Midori's bin. I'm going through a whole stack of them at my desk, tearing out any pictures I like. "It's charging in the kitchen."

That's what I usually do now. If it's closer than that, it's just too tempting to grab it for one last look, and if Nana catches me, my phone goes away for days.

Nana nods. "We had a big day, didn't we? But all that action means I'm super tired. I'm going to get into bed and read."

Before she can turn away, I say, "Nana?"

She stops and looks at me.

"I was thinking. If we buy this house, we'd have that extra bedroom downstairs."

Nana rubs her chin. "That's true."

"If Mom wanted to visit, there'd be a room for her to stay in. It wouldn't be a problem. She'd have her own space."

Nana doesn't look surprised when I say this. Far from it.

She doesn't look sad and old, either, the way she used to.

She hop-hops in and sits down on my bed.

"You'd like to see your mom again, wouldn't you, honeybee?" She waits for me to nod before she goes on. "I'm glad you feel

253

that way. My feelings about your mom are a little more complicated. I haven't changed my mind about her needing to be in treatment if she wants to stay with us."

I let the magazine flop closed. I'm making up my mind about something, something I've been thinking over for a while. "You know where Mom is, don't you?"

Nana runs her hands through her hair and suddenly looks like Albert Einstein.

"Is she in Salt Lake City?"

"*Franny!* Have you been snooping around in my room again?"

"It was the postcard, Nana. The one from Salt Lake City. We don't know anyone there. That's what I thought at first. And then I started thinking, maybe we do."

"I wasn't lying when I said I don't know where your mom is." Nana sighs. "She has a post office box in Salt Lake. I guess it's the closest thing she has to a home base. She has a van and she travels most of the time. She's on disability and she picks up odd jobs and I think that's how she gets by. I started hearing from her a few years back. I didn't tell you, because I was worried she'd disappear again. It's usually postcards, and I don't get them very often. I don't know much more than that."

"Does she ever want to know anything about me?"

Nana pauses. "Questions make your mom nervous. She doesn't like answering them, and she doesn't ask them either. She knows I'd tell her if anything was wrong with you."

It hurts a little to hear that.

Doesn't Mom wonder how I'm doing?

But maybe she does wonder. Maybe there's something else that stops her from asking. Maybe she's embarrassed. Maybe she thinks *I'm* embarrassed.

"Could *I* send Mom a postcard?"

Nana stares fiercely at the window blind like the right answer is written there. Then she says, "Okay."

I jump out of my chair. "Nana! You mean it?"

Nana holds up a finger and stops me short. "As long as you show me what she sends you."

I think about that. "And you show me anything she sends *you*?"

Nana hesitates.

"That's just fair, Nana!"

"Hold on, young lady, give me a moment. Let me think." Her hands are in her hair again. She says, at last, "All right."

Then she lets me hug her. She slumps back against the headboard. "All those questions. I'm too tired to go to bed now!"

She closes her eyes. I look at my nana, with her Rutgers sweatshirt and her faded red pajama pants, and then I climb onto the bed and settle in next to her. She puts her arm around me. You know, I'm pretty tired myself. It's been a long day. A long week. A long few months, really. I can feel myself start to drift away. The light is on, and I should get up and turn it off, but I don't. This time, I'll let Nana take care of it. I know at some point she'll grab her walker and stand up. She'll cover me. She'll pull down the shades and turn off the light and close the door. And then she'll go off to her own bed. But she'll be there when I wake up in the morning. The same way I'll be there for her.

WHY YOU SHOULD BE AN ARTIST

THERE'S A QUOTE BY the musician John Lennon that I like: "Every child is an artist until he's told he's not an artist."

Once at school, I was drawing during class. I was drawing the teacher's desk and the chalkboard behind it. Another girl looked over and said, "What is *that*?" This girl's name was Angie and she liked to create elaborate, detailed drawings of creatures like griffins and dragons that looked like they belonged on Dungeons & Dragons cards. Drawing was Angie's thing, the thing that made her feel special. It was the Twinkie in her lunch box she did not want to share. I was embarrassed, and I stopped working on my drawing. It didn't occur to me to ask anyone else whether they liked my drawing. Or, most important, to ask *myself* whether I liked it.

Sometimes it's other people who tell us we're not artists. But it can also be ourselves. We say things to ourselves like:

"Everyone else is better than I am."

"I'm just messing around. I'm not serious. I can't even draw."

"I could never make something good enough to sell, so what's the point?"

We don't ask ourselves some really simple questions about these thoughts. For example:

"Is the point of making art to win contests?"

"Is the point of making art to be better than everyone else? Or even better than *anyone* else?"

"Is the point of making art to become a professional?"

Art doesn't have to be about impressing people and it doesn't have to be about making a living. It doesn't even have to be about being good at it, although if you keep doing it, you will get better at it.

Art can be a pleasure—especially when we give up the strange idea that it only belongs to experts. It makes us feel good to do it and it's good for us to do it. (Like exercise, making art is good for your brain. Look it up if you don't believe me.) It can even help us figure out what we think or how we feel about complicated things, the way it helps Franny. It looks as if making art was one of the very first things our ancestors did once they had time and energy for anything more than basic survival. Recently, archaeologists found a drawing of a pig on an Indonesian island, Sulawesi, that they estimate to be at least 45,000 years old. When that artist (or artists) painted that pig on Sulawesi so many years ago, I'm willing to bet they did not think, *It's not real art if no one will buy it.*

(Although maybe even then they looked over at someone else's picture and thought, *Everyone else's is better than mine.*)

Art can be all the stuff many of us think of when we imagine artists at work. Things like drawing, sculpting, blowing glass, and making ceramics. But it can be other things too. Things that you can do even if you think you're no good at art. Things that you may already do. Maybe you like to dye eggs in the spring, or decorate your own wrapping paper, or you've yarn-bombed a tree in your yard. If you have—you're an artist already. If you haven't, why not? Art is fun and calming and inspiring, and it's definitely not just for "real artists."

One of my favorite American artists is Ruth Asawa, who made amazing wire sculptures that are now in some of the world's finest museums and private collections. But Ruth didn't just make "serious" sculptures that people would praise and write articles about and pay a lot of money for. She liked to make things out of baker's clay, the way Franny does. This is a humble material found in preschools and summer camps everywhere. You can make it yourself out of cheap ingredients you could probably find in your own kitchen this minute. Ruth did not think this humble material was just for amateurs. She found it inspiring and took it to new levels. This is one of the reasons, among many, I admire her so much. If you are interested in messing around with baker's clay, you can find detailed directions for making, baking, and decorating it at Ruth's website: ruthasawa.com/resources/bakers-clay-recipe.

I hope you give it a try.

ACKNOWLEDGMENTS

Many thanks to my agent, Rachel Orr. I feel really lucky that we ended up on this trip together. The same goes for my editor, Erica Finkel, and to the whole Abrams/Amulet team who worked on *Lost Kites and Other Treasures,* especially Emily Daluga, Kaitlin Severini, Diane Aronson, Megan Carlson, Micah Fleming, Rachael Marks, Maeve Norton, Maggie Lehrman, and Andrew Smith. You all are amazing and I appreciate your hard work, knowledge, and dedication.

Thanks to Bethany Hegedus, Megan E. Freeman, Kate Albus, Nancy Tandon, Joanne Fritz, and Jaime Berry, for excellence above and beyond. Big thanks to my own group of Aunt Gracies—Susan Cohen, Melissa Wish, Peggy Duggan, Trudy Lewis, John Picard, and Jen Richmond. None of you smell like gravy unless you're trying to do so.

Thanks to Tom and Emily Wittmann and Allison Darrow for making sure the Jersey Italian American flavor was right. You deserve boxes of the best Italian pastry—or else thin-crust pizzas. Thanks to Jen Bowen and Adrienne Kane Monroe for helping with the details of Nana's knee injury and rehabilitation, and to Jill Kimball, who shared her art expertise.

Many thanks, and much love, to Bill and Nick—my priceless family.

When I was writing this book, several people—from close friends to acquaintances—shared with me their personal or family stories of mental illness, especially bipolar disorder. Some of them read the book front to back to make sure it was a fair and realistic treatment of one family and that family's situation. Those people did not want to be mentioned here by name, but I remember their generosity and honesty, and I thank them.

ABOUT THE AUTHOR

CATHY CARR WAS BORN in western Nebraska and grew up in Wisconsin. Since high school, she has lived in four different U.S. states, plus overseas, and worked a variety of jobs, from burger flipping to technical writing. Wherever she goes, her observations of the natural world give her inspiration. Her first book, *365 Days to Alaska*, was called "a wonderful debut novel about compassion, belonging, and finding your way home" by Lynne Kelly, author of *Song for a Whale*. It was a Junior Library Guild selection and a Bank Street's Best Children Book of the Year. Cathy lives in the New Jersey suburbs with her family and a semi-feral cat named Barnaby. Visit her online at cathycarrwrites.com.